Charlie couldn't resist sliding a sideways glance to look at his shoes and pants. Expensive jeans and Italian loafers, hardly Seth's laid-back denim-and-sneakers look, but the man was the right height and build. Long, slim legs, big feet.

Finally, she met his eyes and was startled. Different face but same blue-gray orbs, the same color eyes that had met hers intimately, but there was a total lack of recognition and an expression she'd never seen in Seth's eyes.

She looked at his hair. Same color, same hairline, but different style, so again…a good likeness, but nothing she could say was definitively Seth. Her insides churned as she looked, compared, scanned and found only glimpses of someone she might have known intimately.

He looked across the table inquisitively. "So?"

Charlie shook her head. "I don't know. I don't believe we've met." She could swear he looked disappointed. "Give me a few minutes, though." Then she cursed herself for dropping her guard and letting him see she cared, even a little.

Don't get suckered into this man's d[illegible] need it, and he probably wouldn't apprec[illegible]

He knew—he had to—that she wa[illegible] something out of the ordinary. He [illegible] little longer than she'd anticipated. "A[illegible] on't know me?"

Damn. She shook her head agai[illegible] me hands holding hers. Different fa[illegible] is be? It wasn't fair! She tugged gentl[illegible] hand in his.

"No." His voice was insistent [illegible] ding, not threatening. "Please, if you think we've [illegible]. If you have any idea…I need to know."

She pulled again and finally was free of his touch. "You don't look anything like the man I knew."

BOBBIE COLE

is the author of dozens of short stories, confessions and magazine articles, as well as a few dozen novels and novellas under various pseudonyms (both male and female). When she's not writing or spending time with loved ones, she's either curled up with a book, her dogs, good music and some form of beverage, or she's traveling. Upcoming adventures on her agenda include free-falling, zip lining and stomping grapes at a winery—she wants to see her purple footprints on a T-shirt.

MEMORIES OF YOU

BOBBIE COLE

If you purchased this book without a cover you should be aware that this book is stolen property. It was reported as "unsold and destroyed" to the publisher, and neither the author nor the publisher has received any payment for this "stripped book."

Recycling programs for this product may not exist in your area.

ISBN-13: 978-0-373-06249-2

MEMORIES OF YOU

Copyright © 2011 by Bobbie Cole

All rights reserved. Except for use in any review, the reproduction or utilization of this work in whole or in part in any form by any electronic, mechanical or other means, now known or hereafter invented, including xerography, photocopying and recording, or in any information storage or retrieval system, is forbidden without the written permission of the publisher, Harlequin Enterprises Limited, 225 Duncan Mill Road, Don Mills, Ontario M3B 3K9, Canada.

This is a work of fiction. Names, characters, places and incidents are either the product of the author's imagination or are used fictitiously, and any resemblance to actual persons, living or dead, business establishments, events or locales is entirely coincidental.

This edition published by arrangement with Harlequin Books S.A.

® and TM are trademarks of the publisher. Trademarks indicated with ® are registered in the United States Patent and Trademark Office, the Canadian Trade Marks Office and in other countries.

www.CarinaPress.com

Printed in U.S.A.

MEMORIES OF YOU

Acknowledgments and Dedications

This book is for authors Heather Rae Scott & Carla Cassidy.

With much love and appreciation to fellow writers and lakeside campers Gretchen Jones, Pepper Trebuchet & Heather Snow. May you always have an abundance of laughter, cute shoes and great coffee at your disposal.

To editors Angela James and Melissa Johnson, my gratitude for your time, patience and knowledge.

And last, but not least, I wouldn't be writing at all without the love and support of Joshua & Jessica Cole.

Thank you, friends, family and believers.

CHAPTER ONE

NEVER HAD THE SOUND of a man's voice done more healing and more damage than Seth's. Charlie had been excited, despite the anger she'd felt for months, when she first heard him and all he'd done was say hello.

Now he was being a jerk. How dare Seth act like he didn't know who she was?

Charlie hadn't been this close to tears since she'd been shot, and even then she'd steeled herself against the pain, but this was different. This was a pain that stabbed her in places no one could see and reverberated throughout her entire being, making her physically weak and psychically vulnerable, feeling as if she could trust no one, not even herself. And Charlie was nothing if not self-contained.

The sexy male voice on the other end of the line was the cherry on the cake of Charlie's day.

First her captain had saddled her with a new partner, police rookie Julio Rodríguez, who had a bad case of glamour-cop-itis. He wore mirror-shaded sunglasses and sported thick, wavy hair that was too long on top and too short on the sides, and Charlie wouldn't have put it past him to have had a life-sized poster of *CHiPs* star Eric Estrada on his bedroom wall. He'd done his best to charm her with his twenty-six-toothed smile and beefy arm muscles that he flexed at every opportunity. He'd talked her ears off all during their shift, and he'd chided her on the amount of coffee she'd drunk during the hours they were together.

"Green tea, Vargas. You need to treat your body more like a temple than a garbage dump," he'd said at one point. "And feed it. You can't subsist on coffee beans and water. You're gonna give cops a bad name, those of us who like to take care of ourselves."

She'd leveled him with her best go-to-hell stare, and he'd shut up for all of five minutes. Good thing. She'd been about to tell him the tight pants he wore must be cutting off the circulation to his brain if he thought his comments would win his new partner over.

Later, she'd discovered her favorite deli had closed, her bank had inadvertently overcharged her on a bank draft that wasn't hers but someone else's with a similar name, and now a former lover was calling, acting as if he didn't know who she was.

She sat for a moment, stilling her racing pulse and reentering the conversation with Seth Taggart.

"Pardon me?" She knew she sounded edgy, and she'd have liked nothing better than to approach her ex-boyfriend with an air of confidence rather than one of indignation.

The man repeated his questions. "Who are you, and how did I get your number?"

Sputtering, she hung up on him, knowing that if she didn't, she'd tell him where to go and how to get there as quickly as possible.

Fuming, she felt her face flame and was glad Rodríguez had left for the day. Nothing would mortify her more than to burst into tears like some sophomoric fluffball in front of him, and if she didn't monitor her hurt and anger, crying was imminent.

She finished changing out of the sweats she'd worn while working out in the on-site gym after her shift and into her favorite pair of skinny jeans and a cotton V-neck sweater. Running tense fingers through her short hair, she bit her lips to keep them from trembling.

Who am I? You jerk. Just the woman you dated every night for two weeks solid and boldly—and probably insincerely—proposed to the last time you were together.

Charlie plopped to the bench in the dressing room and jerked on her sneakers. She stared at the cell phone beside her as it vibrated, scooting across the bench. Same number, one she hadn't recognized, but she sure remembered the voice.

"Look," she said, not giving the caller a chance to speak. "I don't know where you get off with this attitude after all we've been through, but it's been over a year, you are not funny and I am soooo over you, buster."

She paused, listening, despite the instincts that told her to hang up on him again.

"Is that my name, or is buster what you're calling me to keep from calling me bastard? Because I get the impression you want to rip my head off." The man's voice still sounded familiar, but it held a ring of uncertainty she hadn't heard the first time he'd called, before she'd hung up on him.

Charlie blinked. He didn't sound like a prank caller. What if it really wasn't Seth? What if she'd dreamed of the day he'd phone for so long that this was wishful thinking? "Who is this?" she finally asked, horrified at the possibility that she'd been so rude to someone she didn't know, someone who may have simply needed her assistance.

"That's what I wanted to ask you once you explained who you are."

"Say what?" Charlie did her best to recover quickly, but her heart beat rapidly, and her breath became shallow. *Am I hallucinating? Maybe this is someone I've already helped or at least have spoken to, a man who has my business card.*

Think, Charlie, think, she told herself. *He wouldn't have your personal phone number off your business card.* But someone at the switchboard might have transferred him to her cell phone. Would that show up, though?

Taking her best cop tone, she asked, "What does the card read? Surely you didn't just pull my name out of thin air."

He appeared to be either concentrating or searching, because he was quiet a moment before speaking. Then that same sexy voice unnerved her again. "There isn't a card."

Well, that settles that. She tried picking up the fractured thread of conversation once again. "So why are you calling me?"

"I was in a car wreck some time back, and this number is the only thing I remember prior to the accident. Just the number. It's been playing over and over in my head, like a movie I can't forget, so I phoned." Then he sounded agitated. "This isn't a crank call—I really need to know who you are."

Impatiently, and still thinking of Seth Taggart, she demanded, "No, you called me. Who are you and how did you get this number? I haven't had it but over a year."

"I-I don't know. That is, I'm not sure. All I know is that it keeps playing in my head and that I can't remember a damn thing else. I figured it had to mean something."

She heard him take a deep breath, and she wondered at his serious tone. If this was Seth, he had a hell of a nerve. Sure, they'd only seen one another a few times, but those days and nights had been magical. They'd met at her favorite pub one night after she was off work. They'd talked for hours, and he'd walked her home...then kissed her.

She still remembered the feel of his arms about her, how well their bodies had seemed to fit, with her much smaller, shorter frame molding to his taller one. He'd smelled of a delicious aftershave. His lips had been firm but soft, and his breath had tasted of peppermint and wine. His natural scent was a masculine mix of woodsy testosterone and urban sophistication, as if he belonged nowhere and everywhere.

She groaned. Why hadn't she kept from telling him the truth about her job that night? They'd both been reluctant to exchange more than names, wanting to get to know one another in other ways and leave the superfluous surface stuff for later. Their romance had been intoxicating, exciting, passionate and all-consuming. She hadn't been that head-over-heels giddy since she'd been a college sophomore, but even then, the relationships she'd had seemed superficial compared to what she'd felt with Seth.

He finally spoke. "My name, or so they tell me, is Mason Aldridge, and…I think they're lying to me."

Was he kidding? Personal feelings warred with cop instincts. "When you called before, I thought you sounded like a guy I knew…well. That's why I was mad at you and thought you were yanking my chain."

"I'm not playing games with you." His voice sounded troubled.

Charlie couldn't help but take hope. "Where are you? Who is lying to you?"

"I'm in Houston now—and I know this sounds ludicrous. My sister and her husband, the doctors, all of them. I don't think I'm who they say I am, but it doesn't make sense that they'd help me live a lie."

Charlie's heart sank. Seth Taggart had been an only child. He'd told her as much that first week. But then he'd also not gone by the name Mason Aldridge. The only thing she really hadn't known about Seth was his occupation. For some reason, they'd both been hesitant to talk business until that last night, when she'd come clean with him regarding her own.

She had a good reason. Every man she'd dated after she'd graduated from the academy had run like a rabbit once he discovered she was a cop, and she'd been one for the past ten years, ever since she was twenty-one.

Then she'd confessed to Seth, who had seemed fine, even intrigued, but they'd had to part before he divulged his personal information.

At the time, it hadn't mattered because they had a date planned for later in the week after he returned from a business trip. Charlie had great people instincts and skills—they'd served her well as a cold case investigator. She knew he wasn't involved in anything illegal or immoral. She just knew it.

"Are you originally from Houston, Mr. Aldridge?"

"Call me Mason, please. I think so. I've gone through all of my personal papers. My birth certificate tells me I was born here, but I actually live north of the city, closer to Alvin."

More reason not to consider Seth, who had told

her he hailed from Chicago, that his parents had been killed when he was ten and that he'd been raised by an aunt in Port Charles, Louisiana.

"I see."

"Look, I don't mean to be rude," he interjected, "but I really need to know who I'm talking to and how we met. Does my name ring a bell?"

"No, I'm afraid not." Charlie struggled to maintain professionalism. "I'm a cop. Sometimes people think of something they'd forgotten after we talk, but your name doesn't strike any cords. I'm sorry. I'll check my files." She had another thought. "How long have you had my number? Does the name Seth Taggart mean anything to you?"

"I don't know. And, no. The name means nothing."

Charlie latched onto his first response. "You don't know how long you've had my number?" She knew she sounded incredulous.

Again, the momentary silence on his end before he spoke. The man's caution while feeding her information piecemeal drove her nuts. His next words, however, weren't confusing—they were shocking… and compelling, filling her once again with hope.

"I woke up in a Mexican hospital a year ago last December after a thunderstorm, and all I know is that the other driver didn't survive the car crash and that I don't recognize my face in the mirror, my name or anything about my life. Your number is the only thing that seems familiar to me, and now that

I'm mobile, I want to meet you, to see if you recognize me and if you can help me."

There it was, finally, the reason he'd initially called. Charlie had a knot forming in her stomach that didn't dissolve, only grew tighter and bigger as possibility warred with doubt. She couldn't help but wonder. Was it possible he was really Seth and just didn't know it?

She searched her memory. The last time they'd been together, she'd just gotten the number. Her old phone had broken, and she hadn't wanted the same carrier. Policy with the new phone company had dictated that she get a new number. She had definitely given it to Seth.

If he'd had a visit to Mexico planned, however, she hadn't known because he hadn't told her where he was going the last time she saw him, just that it was business-related. There was only one way to find out.

Charlie told him to get a pen, and she gave him the location of the first place they'd had dinner, a hole-in-the-wall, family-run Tex-Mex restaurant east of the city. It was about a mile from the local police station and not too far for either of them to drive.

"Great." He sounded sincere, but his tone lacked enthusiasm. "What time?"

"Tomorrow, noon. Don't be late."

"I won't." With that, he hung up, leaving her both devastated and excited.

If he was Seth, maybe he had a head injury—sure

sounded like him. If it wasn't the man she knew, she'd try remembering when she'd given this guy who'd just phoned her number. She'd need to search her files to see which case she'd been on from the previous January or February through summer, since he said he'd had it for some time, and with an amnesiac, "some" could be God knew how long.

Odds were that this was just a man she'd come across who may or may not have had information she needed pertaining to a case.

In the meantime, she'd get on the internet and call in some favors, and research car crashes in Mexico, not that she had much to go on. Aldridge hadn't specified where or precisely when he'd been involved in the wreck.

Charlie finished dressing, grabbed her shoulder bag and left, deciding she needed a drink before going home to her empty apartment.

MASON WALKED about the house after he hung up. He hadn't recognized the woman's voice, and she certainly hadn't seemed eager to speak with him. He was sure she knew him at first though, which raised his hopes, especially after that little catch in her voice when she'd indicated that she'd known him well. If he'd left such a bad impression, however, maybe it was a mistake to request a meeting with her, especially if she was a woman with a mad-on and a gun.

Every cell in his system screamed for parole from

the self-imposed prison he'd constructed. What bugged him most was that he resented himself for being unable to express what he felt, and there were times when he truly had emotions that begged for release.

Granted, quite often what he experienced was confusion, anger, even rage, at not knowing precisely what he felt. Most of the time, though, what ailed him was the loneliness, because in his gut he knew there were missing pieces, people, and that those people had names he couldn't recall.

Stupid, he surmised, to get irked simply because he didn't have a soul to talk to that he trusted. There were probably millions of people who lacked opportunity for relationships, folks who didn't have the financial means to secure what they wanted or needed.

Unlike me. The astronomical amount of money he had at his disposal didn't comfort him, though. If anything, he considered it yet one more reason not to trust whoever tried getting close to him, which brought up another problem for him to mull.

If he didn't trust himself and had no solid reason to rely on others to be with him for his wit, personality, charm or the usual social, philosophical, ethical or moral attributes most people were attracted to, what was the use of mingling, of going out, of attempting to get close to anyone else?

It had taken him months to convince himself to call the number that had played in his mind for so long. Logic dictated that the sequence of numbers was a mere random thought, nothing of consequence. It had seemed irrational to be so obsessed over it, but a thin thread of emotional attachment had wound its way into his psyche, ultimately overpowering him, urging him to call and get it over with, to put his mind at ease, even if whoever answered the phone thought he was nuts.

He'd intended to be apologetic when the owner of the phone answered, but the decidedly feminine voice had unnerved him, not in a bad way but definitely throwing his emotional state into one of unbalance and unease. He hadn't meant to be so blunt, to force the issue the way he had. His problem shouldn't be anyone else's, but now that he'd reached out and sought help, the lady cop was involved. He wondered what she looked like.

"Snap out of it," he muttered, turning down yet another long, winding corridor. "She could be old enough to be your mother."

The mansion's interior seemed cold, impersonal, pristine but unimaginative. He didn't remember the house, not a single room in it. He couldn't recall the faces in the pictures that stared back at him from photograph albums in the library and portraits lining various halls.

Now and then the cook would prepare a meal that resonated, but even then...not too deeply. It was if he'd remember the taste of the food she prepared but not necessarily the meal itself.

Mason didn't even remember his sister, the

woman with the pinched face and troubled eyes who seemed to both loathe and fear him. Her husband, Doug, was no better. Evidently, his father had left Mason the house with instructions that his sister was given license to live there if she so desired, and Dorinda definitely wanted. In fact, she'd been up his ass twenty-four/seven, and he couldn't fathom why, because it certainly wasn't because they enjoyed one another's company.

He couldn't call for take-out without her chiming in her order. Mason couldn't go for a drive without her asking the staff where he was headed, then grilling the chauffeur afterward.

It had taken him weeks after Dorinda and Doug had brought him back to the States before he realized the house was truly his and that he didn't owe her the time of day, much less an accounting of his whereabouts. Didn't stop the two of them from keeping tabs on him, though.

His hand reached into the soft chinos encasing his legs and felt for his cell phone. The metal felt warm against his palm, familiar and trustworthy, attributes he didn't feel for any of the people in his life, and he wondered how long he'd been so jaded. Was he this way prior to the accident, or had he only since then developed an innate fear of living in his own skin? He hated feeling out of control and second-guessing his own personality.

Mason rolled his thumb over the small, smooth ball on the cellular device. Just knowing that someone—even if it was a woman who clearly held disdain for him—was out there, within a phone call's reach and that she possibly held news that could enlighten him, gave him a small slice of comfort.

He'd come to realize he craved human contact yet felt as if it was foreign to his nature, which gave him more reason to wonder about the kind of man he must've been before waking up from the coma with a face he didn't recognize. Who in their right mind could turn their back on connecting with others, especially if they sounded like the woman he'd spoken to tonight?

So many questions, so few people he could ask. The Mexican police had been no help. Of course, when he'd been in the coma, he'd been at his sister's mercy and was lucky, if her demeanor was any indication, that she hadn't pulled his life support plug. The police in Guadalajara had no interest in him. To them, he was merely a guest who frequently stayed at a villa offshore and attended business meetings with others in the same field.

Mason snorted. What field? The company with his name on it was strange, unknown to him. He didn't remember any of the people there and had no clue how to run the damned thing.

Memory problems aside, he hoped—if not knew—that somewhere in the recesses of his brain, there was a much more interesting fellow than someone who simply oversaw the production of products that did nothing to further a living planet and whose contribution to the community was only to employ several hundred people to manufacture dishes with lids.

He'd spent several hours in the mansion's library, going through Jasper Aldridge's personal papers. He admired the old man's spunk and ability to build a company from a warehouse to a complex of buildings with considerable staff by the time he died at age seventy. But while Jasper had carved a niche in an already burgeoning market, Mason didn't identify with him on any level. Not on a personal one, nor a business one. He'd look at Jasper's photo and feel only a hollow pit where he suspected a son's grief should reside.

That was another thing. Who the hell was the woman in the other car, the one who had died? Her name, Marjorie Lawson, meant nothing to him, yet her face seemed familiar. The weird thing was that he could visualize her as if he'd been sitting next to her. For some reason, he kept seeing her profile when he'd close his eyes, trying to remember all he could of Mexico. But if she'd been the other driver, how was it possible that he could recall her profile?

Mason had researched, telephoned and written to various government offices in both Texas and Mexico to no avail. Nobody could tell him more than the woman's name, and even that sounded contrived. Not that he'd have known her. She was just some woman who had apparently crashed into his sister's car upon their leaving a business dinner. A nobody, the police had told him. None of your business, they'd added. Not his business? After all he'd been through, the surgeries, loss of memory? He had a right to know what and who had caused the accident.

He flipped through the hospital reports that the Mexican authorities had sent, the photographs he'd purchased from a travel agent, and the brochures he'd requested from the hotel where they'd stayed. All had left more questions than they'd given answers.

Maybe this is your life, he told himself. *Maybe you're not as interesting as you'd like to be.*

Restlessly, he set aside the papers and walked across the hall to his bedroom suite. Something didn't feel right—it hadn't for weeks. He told himself it was the house, his room, and that he simply needed to hire a decorator. The thought nearly panicked him, though. If he didn't know who he was or what he liked, what was the sense in spending money to have someone else tell him what he might enjoy?

His frustration built, and he threw open the double doors to his walk-in closet, which was really yet another room, one in which nobody slept, although God knew it was large enough to fit several beds comfortably. Four walls, row after row of suits, French-cuffed shirts, slacks. Floor-to-ceiling shelving with built-in shoe racks, jewelry drawers where watches and rings, tie clasps and cufflinks winked at him. Another set of sliding drawers lay open like a department store display, where silk ties lay neatly arranged by color, darkest at one end and lightest at the other.

Mason blinked, almost blinded by a headache that began at the base of his neck and peaked just behind his eyes. Instead of the pain making him tired, it jump-started his adrenaline. An overpowering feeling of being smothered, closed in or off, something he couldn't pinpoint… What?

"Aargh!" He rubbed his eyes, forehead, cheeks, the back of his neck. What was wrong with him that he couldn't even choose something to wear? Where would he go anyway? Why was it suddenly important for him to leave the house?

He looked…for something…he wasn't sure what. Beautiful clothes all around. Expensive watches, leather shoes. Why couldn't he find what he needed? The more he tried remembering, the weirder he felt, the more uncomfortable, unsure. He hated the feeling. Despised it.

Then he became frantic, searching, opening doors and drawers, shoving hangers aside, growling his frustration, growing angrier with each thrust of his arm against what felt like a concrete wall of well-crafted coats, jackets, suits, whatever his hands came into contact with—he just kept shoving, his voice rising, yelling until he was out of breath and weak with exhaustion.

He stopped, dropped to his knees in the middle

of the large closet, then rolled to his back and closed his eyes, trying to regulate his breathing.

Instead of the impersonal closet ceiling above him, he imagined what he wanted, sunshine and fresh air, a countryside maybe, anything but this. He cocked his head, eyes still closed, listening for his memory to whisper the magic words he felt he was withholding from himself, and if not words maybe simply another sensation. That was it. Touch. Something soft, durable yet warm and inviting, comfortable.

When he opened his eyes, he recognized the cubicle of his self that felt empty, needing filling. His stood and reassessed his surroundings. His eyes raked the interior of the room, looking at the shambles he'd made of it. He finally knew something he must have liked…and missed. Clothing that made him feel comfortable in his own skin. Denim.

"I want to wear jeans." Mason laughed, quietly at first then louder as he realized the breakthrough he'd just made.

Maybe in order to find his true self, he had to peel off the layers of what others had told him made up Mason Aldridge. Made him feel rather like some soulless onion, but he had to start somewhere. Shedding what didn't work seemed the logical path toward finding what did.

Someone rapped softly on the door to his closet.

"Yes?" he called.

Phillip Pink, the butler, entered. "Mr. Aldridge, are you alright, sir?"

Mason nodded, feeling guilty. The old man looked frightened, disbelieving, as his eyes took in the sight.

"Mr. Pink, please tell Hector I wish to go out, but don't let my sister or her husband hear you. Be discreet." The chauffeur and butler were two of the few people Mason trusted. He glanced at his watch. If he didn't leave now, the mall would close before he got there.

Maybe while he was out, he'd have Hector drive past the restaurant where he was to meet…what was her name?

He placed his hands on his hips. Damn it, she hadn't told him. He'd asked her two or three times, but the woman still hadn't given him her name. He had no clue what to say when he entered the restaurant, nothing to give their staff to tell them who he was meeting. Well, hell. Maybe she'd recognize him. Otherwise, how would they connect?

Mason pulled out his cell phone. He could call her again, but the hour was late. She was already in a bad mood. Probably better for him if he just took his chances the next day.

"Mr. Aldridge." The butler interrupted his thoughts. "Are you alright, sir?"

Mason felt a rush of chagrin. He stuffed the cell phone back into his pocket then grinned like a maniac, an expression he was certain Pink had never seen on Aldridge's face. He walked over to the much older man, grasped him by the shoulders and did something that felt freeing but totally out of character. He hugged Pink.

"I will be, Mr. Pink. I will be."

CHAPTER TWO

POMME DE TERRE WAS A SMALL restaurant set against a backdrop of a man-made lake and owned by a Frenchman from Louisiana. Charlie and her college roommates, Gretchen and Heather, had frequented the place for years, so when Charlie had met Seth, and he'd claimed to miss his aunt's cooking from his childhood in Port Charles, Pomme de Terre had seemed the logical place to take him one night when they'd been looking for a place for dinner. The establishment's fare ranged from Tex-Mex to Cajun, and Seth had loved spicy foods.

No reservations were needed, and the atmosphere was conducive to both intimacy and fun. Heather had eventually married Jason Ettienne, the owner's son. It'd be nice to get a second pair of eyes on Charlie's mysterious caller, since both Jason and Heather had met Seth. They could tell her whether she was going bonkers or if the owner of the voice was indeed the man who'd literally gotten away.

Heather, who served as hostess sometimes, happened to be there when Charlie arrived. "Damn, girlfriend, what brings you to the Apple of the Earth in the middle of the week? You just miss me, or do you need a friend?" She pulled Charlie aside from the line of customers to hug her.

Charlie smiled ruefully. "Both." She explained her situation.

Heather's blue eyes grew rounder by the syllable. "Wow. But amnesia? I mean, how else could he explain not knowing who he was?"

Charlie shook her head. "It doesn't make sense—I'm probably just stressed and overly imaginative. Not like I haven't thought of the guy since he split."

"Still. I want to see him." Heather grabbed a couple of menus. "How about facing the lake? It's closer to the office. I want Jason to pop out and have a look, see what he thinks."

"Great." Charlie loved that area of the restaurant. There was something calming about water, and Lord knew she was jittery and needed a panacea of some sort.

She settled into the booth, facing the water, with her back slightly to the entrance where Mason or Seth would enter. Normally, she kept her back to a wall out of cop habit, but this time she trusted her instincts—that Heather would have her back, and Jason, if he was around, was big enough to help if she felt threatened. Not that she did. Yet. However, her stomach churned with anticipation and trepidation. If it was Seth, what would she do? She couldn't very well blast the man for having left her if he had no clue who he was.

Get it together, Charlie. She forced her brain to

switch gears as she thought of what Rodríguez had said about her eating habits. Pain in the butt that he was, he had a point regarding her diet. While food was the last thing on her mind, she opted for iced tea instead of coffee and requested a bowl of crisp tortilla chips and salsa to munch while she waited. Not exactly what Rodríguez would have called healthy food, but she figured it was better than just coffee.

She glanced toward the water a few yards from the elevated restaurant. Instead of looking inviting, it appeared chilly, just like her mood. It would be, she thought, considering the fall weather.

Waves lapped against the rocky shore, and the reflection of autumn leaves that hadn't yet fallen warmed the otherwise crystal blue water, giving it a less ominous presence. Unlike the icy shell her heart had developed. She didn't want to be here, but she was damned if she'd pass up the chance to find out for sure what Aldridge wanted, other than validation.

She tensed, sensing someone approaching, but she steeled herself not to turn.

Heather's voice was clear but professional, masking the hint of curiosity Charlie knew her friend must feel. "I believe this is your party."

Charlie couldn't resist sliding a sideways glance to look at his shoes and pants. Expensive jeans and Italian loafers, hardly Seth's laid-back denim-and-sneakers look, but the man was the right height and build. Long, slim legs, big feet.

She stole a look at his hands as he placed them on

the table, a natural reflex for someone sliding into a booth's bench seat, and she had her first feeling of doubt. Dismayed, she realized she had no clue whether Seth's fingers or hands had held any distinguishing marks. She didn't recall any scars, and this man had none, but it was hardly enough to go on.

Finally, she met his eyes and was startled. Different face but same blue-gray orbs, the same color eyes that had met hers intimately, but there was a total lack of recognition and an expression she'd never seen in Seth's eyes.

She looked at his hair. Same color, same hairline, but different style, so again…a good likeness, but nothing she could say was definitively Seth. Her insides churned as she looked, compared, scanned and found only glimpses of someone she might have known intimately.

He looked across the table inquisitively. "So?"

Charlie shook her head. "I don't know. I don't believe we've met." She could swear he looked disappointed. "Give me a few minutes, though." Then she cursed herself for dropping her guard and letting him see she cared, even a little.

Don't get suckered into this man's drama. You don't need it, and he probably wouldn't appreciate it anyway.

He held out his hand for her to shake. "Mason Aldridge," he said, "but I'm afraid I don't know who you are."

She nodded curtly and gave her name as she took

his hand. It was warm, and her throat went dry at its touch. A flood of sensations washed over her, and she fought hard not to get swept into the storm as memories of Seth assaulted her.

You're just feeling that electrical current pass between the two of you because you are thinking of Seth, she scolded herself.

He knew—he had to—that she was experiencing something out of the ordinary. He held her hand a little longer than she'd anticipated. "Are you sure you don't know me?"

Damn. She shook her head again. Same voice, same hands holding hers. Different face. How could this be? It wasn't fair! She tugged gently, but he kept her hand in his.

"No." His voice was insistent but not commanding, not threatening. "Please, if you think we've met, if you have any idea...I need to know."

She pulled again and finally was free of his touch. "You don't look anything like the man I knew."

"I've had facial reconstruction," he told her.

Charlie's guts twisted. She stared at him openly, long and hard. "Because of the accident?"

"Yes. I don't know who I am, but I know I'm not Mason Aldridge." His face was handsome, but it was as if he were a work of art in progress, not a completed project. It lacked a certain steel, an edge, a depth of pain and experience she'd been expecting. "Aldridge is just a name I use when I introduce myself or sign a check."

"How do you know this? How can you be that positive you aren't Aldridge?" she asked.

"Instinct." He leaned back in his seat. The muscles in his jaw worked, taut skin moving over well-chiseled bones. "Something tells me that we've met. Your face isn't familiar, but your voice is. We were close, intimate, I think. Please, you have to remember, because I can't."

Heather cleared her throat, and Charlie looked up, perturbed but grateful. She needed time to think. Placing their orders would give her the chance to gather her thoughts, choose her words carefully, so she pointed at the menu and gave her choice of entrée.

Charlie reverted to cop, noting her companion's order. Aldridge hadn't even looked at the menu, just asked if they served chalupas. When Heather said yes, he nodded.

No big deal. Lots of people liked that dish.

Then he called Heather back. "I forgot to make a request—double beans, no rice and extra jalapeños. Thanks."

Heather immediately glanced at Charlie and cocked an eye. It was what Seth would have ordered.

Charlie averted her gaze as she thought, and her eyes focused on two men sitting at a booth catercorner from them. Both men were looking at them but quickly turned away as soon as they caught her staring in their direction. She realized she might have been the one being rude and immediately turned her attention back to Heather and Mason.

"Did I say something wrong?" he asked, looking at Charlie.

"What?" She reeled herself back to what he'd said. "Not at all. That's how I get my plate, only no jalapeños." She debated on how much to reveal and decided to keep mum as to Seth's preferences.

"You're spicy enough, heh?" he joked.

Charlie choked and had to reach for her glass of water. Exactly what Seth had said on occasion, teasing her about her quarter-Mexican heritage and not being true Hispanic if she didn't like the hot peppers.

When Heather left, Mason, or whoever he was, leaned forward and spoke quietly. "Let's lay it all out here on the table. All I know is that I'm not trying to get into your pants. I have money—and while this face isn't mine, it's not that bad to look at, right?"

She could tell he wasn't looking for compliments, so she nodded slowly. "No, it's a nice face." She frowned, trying to discern precisely how this face was different from the one she knew. "Have you had cheek implants or an alteration here?" She brushed the back of her hand against her jaw.

"Both, plus a new nose. Evidently, my face was crushed." He sighed. "The doctors in Mexico did their best using a photo my sister provided them."

"Seth Taggart didn't have a sister," Charlie murmured before she could stop herself. Now he had a name.

"Seth," he mused. "Even that doesn't sound right, but it's a start, more than what I had before I arrived. Thanks."

Well, that's not good, not if the sound of his own name doesn't ring any bells. The hope she hadn't realized she'd been building deflated, leaving Charlie feeling once again at a loss. The push-pull conversation wasn't tiring so much as frustrating.

"Charlene—for some reason I want to call you Charlie," he said.

Her eyes widened. "That's my nickname."

"May I call you that?"

"Sure." She squirmed but reminded herself she was a cop, a woman in what for years had been a man's job, so it was natural for anyone with half a brain to segue from the female form of her name to a more masculine nickname.

He continued. "I don't dye my hair—is it the same color as your friend's?"

"Yes." *Weird that he is so analytical and thinks like a cop, but then he's had time to wonder about himself and how he got here since he woke up.*

He persisted. "And the eyes? Even if I've had surgery, those would be the same color, right?"

"Yes, again. They're the same." Exactly the same. Charlie stifled the sigh that threatened to escape as she found herself getting lost in their depths.

"So there's a strong possibility that I'm Seth Taggart. You said you're a police officer? Do you think you could help me check into this man's background, maybe find someone who might have known Seth… or me?"

Charlie sighed. "Been there, done that, I'm afraid." She tossed aside her previous reluctance to get involved. Now she wanted to know, too, for personal reasons. "When you—that is, when Seth disappeared, I followed up on everything he'd told me about himself, which wasn't much."

"Oh." He sounded disappointed. "I was hoping, no offense, that we'd been closer than that." His eyes lowered, and he looked at her mouth then quickly averted his gaze momentarily. "Don't take that the wrong way, please."

She chuckled nervously and decided the present wasn't the time to tell him quite everything. "We only knew one another a few weeks, less than a month."

"I see. What did you find out when you looked for me?"

"I had just told you what I did for a living, and one of the reasons I figured you'd disappeared was because I'm a cop. Most men don't handle that information well. It spooks them."

He nodded but frowned. "Was Seth the type of man who'd mind, do you think? Because that doesn't feel strange to me now, knowing your profession."

"I don't know. He didn't tell me what he did for a living." She shrugged. "I checked hospitals for accident victims." She felt herself blush. "I even ran the databases I have at work, everything from the

Department of Motor Vehicles for a driver's license to Vital Statistics to trace a birth certificate. Nothing."

"That doesn't make sense. I drive...ah."

She finished for him. "You have a license as Mason Aldridge. Seth Taggart didn't have one."

"Didn't he drive to meet up with you when you went out?" he asked.

"No, he was always in the neighborhood or took a cab, and unfortunately, at the time, I never really noticed things like that." She wet her lips, feeling both them and her throat go dry. "Lots of people don't drive. Not many of them are in Texas, but the subject just never came up. I always had a vehicle, he was always on foot or nearby or something when we'd meet up."

"Did you check other states?"

She was aware of the depth of her feelings for Seth with her next statement. Her voice was low, quiet and laced with the anger she'd sat on for months. "All fifty states, Puerto Rico, the Virgin Islands, Guam and the Philippines. I even searched through records for an international driver's license, the kind people get when they travel a lot overseas."

She could tell by the slow smile that lifted the corners of his mouth that the implication she hadn't meant to divulge had registered with him. He knew she'd had a big emotional stake in her relationship with Seth.

"You must've wanted to find this man pretty badly."

"I did, for fifteen months."

"Ah. Which is precisely when my medical records show that I was in the car crash." He looked at her thoughtfully. "Care to tell me more?"

"Don't look so smug," she said, as if he really were Seth. "It's my job."

"But you were dating him, I take it, not looking for him because he owed you money or had committed a crime."

She shifted in her seat, starting to get pissed off the more she thought about Seth. "Can we change the subject?"

He nodded. "If we don't, you'll likely make some excuse to visit the restroom or say you have an important phone call to make. I may have lost my memory, but not my sense of propriety."

Charlie felt a chill of unease but refused to rub her arms or give any indication that she was unnerved. Telling him to discuss something else was enough of a clue that he'd upset her.

True to his word, he brought up another topic, circling back to what he'd previously asked. "Do you think you might help me?"

Easy enough—she was obligated as an officer to help. "I'll do what I can. What would be best would be for you to speak with someone at the police department or find a good private investigator and give them all the information you can."

He pulled a small notebook and pen from his jacket and began to scribble until ink appeared. "Do you know of anyone I could call?"

When she didn't readily answer, he looked up. She knew her face must've drained of color. He was a lefty, a southpaw, just like Seth, and he curved his hand the same way around the pen that Seth did.

"What's wrong?" he asked.

Charlie cleared her throat and finally found her voice. "Nothing. I was just thinking."

He gave her a direct look. "You were being a cop. What did I do or say that triggered that look? C'mon, tell me." Then he followed her gaze to his hand with the pen in it. "Was Seth left-handed?"

"Yes, but that doesn't mean anything either. Lots of folks are—"

"What do you mean 'anything either'? There's something else?" he pressed her.

Charlie leaned back. "Damn, you don't miss much, do you?"

At that moment, Jason walked up to the table, leaned over and hugged Charlie. "Hey, girl."

"Hey, Jason." Charlie made introductions, glad of her friend's intrusion. It gave her time to assess Mason more carefully while he and Jason spoke. His plastic surgeon had to have been a wizard with a scalpel, because she couldn't see so much as one hair's width scar anywhere on his face, neck or the strong column of throat that was exposed in the V beneath his Adam's apple where his Oxford shirt buttoned.

She felt her lips part as she looked at the smooth, hairless chest, what little of it she could see. Her throat felt dry, parched, as she recalled the nights she'd spent lying against Seth, running her tongue along his collarbone and into the small V, much like Mason's.

Jason only stayed a few seconds, but Charlie could tell he was checking out her companion, looking for anything that might reveal Seth.

After he left, Mason set down the pen. "Did you and I come here often?"

"Quite a bit, considering we didn't know one another that well. That is, if you are Seth Taggart. We don't know that you are."

He nodded. "And the hostess who seated me, and the owner...they're friends of yours, I take it. Did they know Seth?"

"How do you know they're friends of mine?" she asked, turning the tables.

He shrugged. "Maybe I dated a cop and some of her quirkiness rubbed off on me."

Charlie couldn't help but smile. So he wasn't backing down or giving up. Good. The man was growing on her.

"Maybe you were a cop yourself," she said.

He scoffed. "Doubt it."

"How do you know?" she asked.

He splayed his fingers expressively. "Just makes

sense. Because if I was an officer of the law, there would be fingerprints, a driver's license, some form of public record unless I lived in a hotel, considering I'd have to live somewhere, and they pull a credit file for things like that, have for some time." He paused. "I think."

Charlie sat up straighter as a thought hit her. "What do you know about police work?"

"I have no idea. That just popped out as we were talking. Surely, if I'd been in the same line of work as you, though, I'd have mentioned it once you told me your job."

"Unless you were I.A.," she said.

"Internal Affairs? Why would I be checking up on you?"

He's doing it again. Another chill swept over her. For someone who didn't know much about himself, he had an uncanny ability to drift in and out of law enforcement jargon with ease, and he certainly had a ready answer, a comeback that thrust the questions back upon her, giving him the opportunity to avoid answering something himself. Just like Seth, now that she thought of it.

"You said something I haven't tried." She indicated his water glass, still full. "When you're finished with that, why not let me run your fingerprints though AFIS?"

"Sure." He took one sip and then another. "Just don't let them refill the glass. No matter who or what

I am, I'm sure my body has limits on how much it can hold."

She fished in her purse. "No need." She brought out tape and a plastic bag and secured the prints she wanted.

Mason cleared the table, making room for his plate when their food arrived. Charlie did the same. She glanced back toward the table where the two men had been watching them and frowned. They were still staring, but they both lowered their eyes again and went back to talking as soon as they saw that she noticed them.

"What, or who, are you looking at?" Mason asked, turning in his seat.

Charlie was about to say something when she saw his face, the way he scrutinized the two men. Just as a cop would have done, his eyes covering middle then top then bottom and back to their midsections, where most men carried their guns, somewhere strapped to their upper thighs or around the chest, if not within an inside a pocket.

"Maybe we're on to something," she admitted.

"You've aroused my curiosity again," he told her. "Why do you say that?"

She told him, following with another thought. "Let's check. Work with me?"

"Sure."

She leaned forward and quietly asked, "What are they wearing, and what are their ages?"

His gaze never wavered. He seemed not to flinch

or even consider turning around for another look. It was if he channeled someone or went into a clear-minded trance as he spoke. "Stouter man is about five-eleven, weight of two-ten, balding head, non-descript brown jacket that doesn't go with the black shoes. I'd say he's in his mid-forties, as is his buddy."

He took a quick breath. "The guy facing us sits about two inches higher, so he's taller or has a taller torso. Same shoes, blue shirt with a small diamond pattern and dark jacket." He perked up. "The shoes—both pair look like standard uniform fare, like for someone not undercover. Right?"

Charlie grinned, unable to contain her excitement. "You're either someone with a military background, you're involved in law enforcement or you're an interior decorator. Whichever, you have good powers of observation."

He smiled back. "Nothing to bank on, but I'll take it. Thanks." He took another long drink from his water glass and set it down. "Crap."

"What?" She stiffened, expecting something she wouldn't like to hear.

He held out his hands, palms up. "I forgot. I burned my hands and fingertips somewhat in that wreck. Will it matter much?"

She sighed. "Won't know until we get back to the station."

"How long do you think it'll take to run the prints on this?"

"Matter of hours if we catch my friend Carla on duty."

"Then let's eat quickly," he suggested. "And no staring at me to see if I do this or that like Seth would have done. I'm self-conscious enough."

Charlie bit her lip to keep from smiling again. She realized she'd been concerned about being the one under scrutiny, never thinking of her companion's worries. She'd entered the restaurant wondering how she'd handle his neediness but hadn't considered her own emotional state. Now she was drawn into a situation she hadn't bargained for, one of giving a damn about him if he wasn't Seth.

I don't, she told herself. Then honesty kicked her. *Well, maybe a little.*

He insisted on paying for her meal once they'd finished eating, telling her he was a man of means, and while he did so, with a gold credit card she recognized but figured she'd never own, she scoured the restaurant for the two men. To her surprise—and then again, not, considering how they'd stared—they were leaving, closing in on them.

She touched his arm and whispered. "Don't go to your own car. Come with me, but hurry."

After he collected his card and receipt, she led him through the kitchen, out the back entrance. He seemed to sense the urgency and didn't ask questions, merely followed closely on her heels. When they got to the rear entrance where supplies were delivered, she led him around to her own car and motioned for him to get inside.

Once there, she asked where he'd parked then slowly pulled around to within a few yards of the expensive sedan.

"Who's that beside the car?" she asked.

"Hector, my driver." At her surprised look, he added, "I told you—I have money."

"Guess so."

"Why all the secrecy?" he asked. "You've already pulled my fingerprints with the tape you had in your bag. I've told you I'd let you swab my mouth at the station—but I'll need to tell Hector so he can follow us."

"Hector will have to do with a phone call. Just wait."

Sure enough, the two men got into a car and waited, and they seemed to be watching the sedan, waiting for someone to get inside and for it to pull out.

"I think you're being followed," she said.

Mason's shoulders squared and his face hardened. He asked her to point them out. "The men from the restaurant?"

"Yep. Any idea who they are?"

"If I'd noticed what they were wearing and didn't comment on their faces, then, no. But now I'm wondering why they're watching me."

"Maybe you're a spy," she joked halfheartedly, praying to God she wouldn't find herself shackled to him like some moll to a gangster or a bimbo to James Bond.

She fished out her cell phone and punched a number. When Heather answered, Charlie asked her, “Are you still smoking?”

“What?” Heather shrieked. The pause on the other end of the line was brief. “You know Jason told me to quit when we started a family.”

“Heather, I don’t care, I just need to know. Please—it’s important.”

“Damn, Charlie,” Heather huffed. “If you wanted a smoke, why didn’t you say something while you were here? Where are you now?”

“I’m in the parking lot, and I need you to take a smoke break. Go out the south door, light up and walk around to your left. Hurry.”

Heather grumbled, but Charlie could hear the rustle in the background.

“This is a new pack, and if Jason catches me, my ass is grass—and so is yours if he chews me out,” Heather told her.

Pretty soon Charlie saw her exit the building and look around. “Go to your right, honey, I’m sorry, not your left. See that gray Lexus across the drive?”

“Yeah.”

“Walk over there like you’re talking to me.”

“I am talking to you, dumbass.”

Charlie couldn’t repress the grin. “Thanks. I owe you one.”

"I am in clear view of Jason's office, Charlie. He's going to catch me."

"Well, tell him I asked a favor and that you had to bum a cigarette from a customer. He'll understand." Charlie watched the two men in the car closely. "Walk around to their west side and act like you've spotted someone you know. Wave."

"To you?"

"No! Like you see someone you know just beyond that Lexus where those men can't see who you're flagging down."

Heather groaned. "With a phone in one hand and a cigarette in the other, I'm to wave? Do I say anything, shout, do more than just look like an idiot saying hello to an empty parking lot across the street?"

Charlie could tell that Mason was amused, but thankfully he wasn't the talkative sort. "Heather, you're doing great. Those men are following us—rather they're following Se—Mason. I need you to use your camera on the phone and take a shot of their car tag, whatever you can get me. Just keep talking and walking around, smoking, and acting like you're on a break from work."

"Crap." Heather walked where Charlie had directed. "I'm hanging up now so I can take the photos."

"Great. Send them to my personal email address, not my work."

Her friend seemed to have forgotten she was to be

covert. Heather looked in Charlie's direction, frowning, and for a moment Charlie was afraid the two men would spot her and follow her gaze.

Charlie pulled out slowly and told Mason to hunker down in his seat. She ignored the two men and Heather, acting as if she hadn't seen them, and whipped around a corner and into the main flow of traffic onto a nearby street.

Whoever they were, they wouldn't be following a car they weren't concerned about and didn't recognize.

"Interesting," was all her companion said.

Charlie took it as a compliment. "Ten years, most of it working cold cases, but my father was a cop. It's in the blood to be suspicious."

MASON KNEW without being told that once they were at the station, he wouldn't be allowed past certain checkpoints. He asked if there might be a book with photos of missing persons to see if he recognized himself, though, and Charlie told him sure. Then she asked if he'd care to browse information or photos concerning the accident in Mexico if she could pull them up on the computer.

It was what he'd prayed for.

He acquiesced to a sample of his DNA as well as the fingerprints then settled into a comfortable chair in a remote corner of an unoccupied interrogation room with a stack of books while he waited on Charlie to come back with whatever she could find.

He figured it'd take several hours, not mere minutes before she returned, and he planned on delving into grisly photos and a mixture of Spanish and English reports, but she was back quickly, and the look on her face told him the news wasn't good.

"Am I a mass murderer or an interior decorator?" he asked, half-joking but with a fist of dread punching his stomach.

"Maybe worse if my hunch is right. It means we probably won't be able to trace you," she replied, sitting across from him at the table. "Carla had almost an immediate hit on your fingerprints in AFIS, but the DNA, of course, will take much longer. We'll have to come back for that, but I already suspect what it'll tell us."

Anxiety shredded him. "What? Who am I?"

"We still don't know. One lead after another came up with the same response in one form or another—file closed, unable to obtain. We figure you're a Fed."

The news shocked him, seemingly more so than it had her, because her face was pale but not alarmed. Either the pert little blonde before him was a good cop with a poker face, which he highly suspected, or she didn't give a damn, which somehow he doubted. "How about the name?" he asked. "Anything associated with those fingerprints?"

"Nothing on Seth Taggart, but then I've already searched every conceivable database, going back to his birth in Chicago and to his childhood in Port

Charles. Maybe he doesn't exist." She paused. "As for the fingerprints, the database locked up on me. So nothing...yet."

"Do you believe he'd have lied to you about something like that?" Mason's eyes held hers. *Do you think I could have done such a thing?* What he was thinking hung in the air like some invisible blade above both their heads.

Charlene nodded. "He would have if he was undercover, especially if he was FBI or CIA."

Mason rose and walked around to where she sat, and she stood as well, shoving the chair beneath the desk. He watched her throat as she swallowed, and the slight motion inflamed him with the desire he'd had since setting eyes on her in the restaurant. Suddenly he didn't give a damn whether anyone was watching from the other side of the glass wall and he didn't care if she slapped his face. He grabbed her by the shoulders and pulled her toward him, and she didn't resist.

"We're both wondering if I'm the man you were with," he said, his voice rough with a mixture of dread, desire and need. "Let's find out."

The kiss began slowly, with him pressing his lips against hers in what he'd intended to be a sweet, slow connection but what flamed into something else entirely. His tongue parted her lips and explored the interior of her mouth, savoring its sweetness, craving the passion he felt as she responded.

He could tell she was unwilling to wholly let him

past the emotional barriers she'd constructed, but he knew when he had her, the moment she opened herself to him, sighing, even whimpering, as their bodies remembered what his mind couldn't.

Her hands slowly left his forearms and slid upward to his shoulders. For brief seconds she clutched him, digging her nails into him before winding her arms about his neck and embracing him fully.

His legs and groin ached with need, and he had to consciously stop himself before he grabbed her bottom and drew her farther into the embrace, wanting to touch her, mold her and feel her warmth thawing the frozen memories of his past.

The air about them in the small room seemed to freeze in time, with a swirling sensation that threatened to undermine his resolve not to go too far with her in his arms.

"Seth." His name was a whisper on her lips as he abruptly stopped kissing her and put her at arm's length.

He stared at her hopelessly for a moment before speaking. "I guess that answers that."

"What are we going to do? How do we prove who you are if you can't remember and if there's no physical record of your existence?" She sounded terrified, not unsure of him but frightened of the situation.

He wasn't sure if he could move forward on his own with no skills he could remember, no access to information and no one to trust. “I’m more worried about whether or not you’ll be here…with me.”

Charlie nodded. “I’ll stay with you. We’ll work it out.”

CHAPTER THREE

HE'D CALLED HECTOR from his cell phone at Charlie's suggestion, and while it was late, he was tired and he knew she wanted to go home, he had been reluctant to leave the station. He lolled his head against the high-back leather seat as the chauffer drove toward his house, thinking of the past few hours and how he already missed her.

It was as if he'd known her all his life and couldn't remember a day without her or a day with her. It was a maddening situation. He'd wanted to ask her to accompany him, but he'd known she'd turn him down. She'd said she wanted to follow up on a project at work when he'd offered to follow her to her car, but he knew that like him, she also needed to adjust to what they'd discovered. Nothing. And everything.

Surely, he told himself, if he was her errant or missing...whatever...boyfriend or lover, her face and body would have haunted him. How could he have forgotten someone like her if that were the case? For all her candor and control, he suspected a feminine, slightly shy, yielding and giving woman.

She'd worn androgynous dark slacks and shoes, typical of a detective, but the soft crème-colored blouse with the open throat beneath the black business jacket had been pure female.

His thoughts segued to the two men at the restaurant. They made him apprehensive. Who were they and what did they hope to accomplish by following him? If he was indeed a Fed—and that's what they looked like—they'd most likely wonder what he was up to, who he'd talked to, why he hadn't contacted them, and what he knew about whatever situation he'd been involved with while in Mexico, since that was where his life had both ended and began. So why, if he was Seth, hadn't they simply rescued him? Was it to keep him in play so he could maybe give them more information later?

Even with the sensations he had experienced kissing Charlene Vargas, he was certain of nothing but one thing: he wasn't Mason Aldridge. He was living in the Aldridge mansion, spending Aldridge money, but he wasn't entitled to it. Without it, though, how would he survive? Definitely a conundrum. Live in luxury as long as he kept his mouth shut or wind up at Charlie's mercy until he figured things out.

"Cheer up," he mumbled to himself. "You could be at a homeless shelter."

"Señor Aldridge?"

Mason looked up, realizing he must've spoken aloud, and he found his driver staring at him in the rearview mirror.

"Sorry, Hector. Just thinking." Mason took a

deep breath, considering his next move. Oh, why not? "Hector?"

"Sí, señor?"

"How long have you known me?"

The driver's eyes widened slightly, but they soon narrowed, troubled, reflecting his hesitancy in answering. "I have worked for your family for about ten years."

"Do I look the same to you now as I did before going to Mexico?" There were only the two of them in the car, so perhaps the chauffeur would level with him. Couldn't hurt.

Hector shook his head. "No. But you and I were never…you know?" He paused. "Buddy-buddy."

Mason picked up on the small thread Hector had inadvertently offered. "Was I a snob or standoffish, or did I treat you badly?"

"Never, Mr. Aldridge. I only meant that we never talk except for you to give me instructions. It's…it's not your family's way." Hector's eyes still looked concerned.

"Do you believe I am Mason Aldridge?" He had to know. "It's not a loaded question. You won't be penalized for being honest. I'm asking because I don't see how, no matter who the others say I am. I don't feel like an Aldridge, and I don't remember anything from a life at the Aldridge mansion, so I want to know how you feel, what you think. Please."

He could see it the moment the man realized he wasn't getting out of answering, at least not gracefully. Hector's shoulders seemed to ease from their tense, subservient but wary, position. He looked at Mason directly via the mirror. "The Mason Aldridge I knew would never have asked me such things. He wouldn't have cared for my opinion, and he would not have said please."

"Then why would my sist—rather the woman posing as my sister—and her husband try convincing me and others that I'm Mason?"

The chauffeur shrugged. "Mason Aldridge—the one I knew—never socialized. He rarely went to his own company, preferring to handle business over the telephone from his home. It wouldn't be that difficult. Weird, yes. Difficult, no."

"Thank you. That's all I needed to know." In that moment, at least in his mind, Mason Aldridge ceased being, and Seth Taggart was reborn. That was the instant Seth reclaimed what little he could decipher of himself, and he made a decision.

And immediately forgot what it was. For a moment, he heard no sound, saw only darkness, couldn't fathom where he was, much less what he was thinking or saying.

"Señor Aldridge?"

Seth rubbed his eyes. What the hell was happening? "What?"

"You mumbled something—I didn't hear what it was." Hector's eyes were narrowed, their expression one of concern. "Are you okay?"

"Oh. Yeah. I remember. Turn around—head back

toward town, please," Seth instructed him. "Hyatt Regency on Louisiana."

Hector immediately found a lane where he could reverse their direction. Without question, he whipped the sedan onto a side street, turned the vehicle around and headed toward a ramp leading to the heart of Houston.

Seth comforted himself with the thought that he had all of the information he needed from the mansion. He'd made copies of documents and put them into a safety deposit box, one of the few things to which Dorinda and Doug Wilkerson didn't have keys.

They could have the run of the mansion, strip it bare and auction off what they couldn't carry to some storage facility—he didn't care. None of it was his, anyway.

Let them wonder where he was until they pried the information from Hector. Something told him, though, that Hector would hold out, that he wouldn't divulge Seth's whereabouts.

He'd phone Charlie the next day and let her know where he was once he secured a room, and he'd have Pink and Hector bring him whatever he needed at the hotel.

As they wound through the business district, a horrific thought struck Seth. Where was the real Mason Aldridge—or his body? He had to be dead if his sister was deliberately trying to pass off any warm body with a crushed face as her brother. And if Hector had figured something was amiss, surely other servants were suspicious. Why hadn't anyone said anything? Was Aldridge that big of an asshole that nobody cared? Or were the servants afraid of Dorinda and Doug?

THE PARTIAL FINGERPRINTS hadn't yielded much, but four points out of ten on the Galton details wasn't bad, Charlie thought, studying the results Carla had given her. Seth must've seared off some of the skin, thereby altering his prints a bit, but there were still enough identifying marks to run, and if he didn't have a set on file before he walked in, he could certainly have one after he left if she was so inclined.

His kiss had left her shattered. She was a small woman, and while it might be unlikely but still possible for a man to overcome her in strength, few had breached her guarded heart, the core of her that lived behind the badge and intellect. She'd learned long ago that whenever that happened, it was time for her to step back, take a second look, a deeper breath, reassess and revise, come up with a plan just in case her emotions became tangled.

If Mason wasn't Seth, there was something seriously wrong with her rationale and her bullshit barometer, because she couldn't find anything to dislike about the man with whom she'd lunched, yet she hadn't discovered anything to love either, nothing other than a kiss she could define as belonging to Seth.

It was as if the Seth she'd known had vanished then reappeared in a different package, and part of what had drawn her to him was the entirety, the whole man, not facets of him. She didn't know what to do with him parceled out to her in a process that required she study and evaluate him one moment, kiss or thought at a time.

She flipped open her cell phone and checked the time. Late, but maybe not too late. She pressed the number two. She was relieved not to get voice mail. "Sam?"

"Yeah?"

She took a deep breath then let it out slowly. "It's me."

"I know who it is. I was there when your mother gave birth to you."

Charlie smiled weakly. "You up for a chat? I need to run something by you."

"You bring the beer, and I'll provide the nachos."

"Be there in twenty minutes."

SHE'D MISSED THE first twenty years knowing her father. His name was Samuel Gordon Vargas, but her mother had always said he was just Sam, which stood for some asshole man. Of course, upon reflection, her mother hadn't been exactly unbiased. Their divorce, like their marriage, had been volatile, and June Vargas hadn't been pleased with the piddly child support a beat cop could deliver back in the day.

Charlene had been named for her paternal grandmother, and while she hadn't any brothers or sisters, she and Sam had never been close. Probably, she figured, because he couldn't stand coming around June, and it wasn't like he could see his daughter without encountering her mother.

June had stopped speaking to her for months when Charlie joined the academy. Her mom still couldn't be in the same room with her more than ten or fifteen minutes without dredging up the past and comparing Charlie's faults to those of her father. Charlie loved her, but June was a cold-hearted, unforgiving, grudge-carrying shrew at times.

Sam, on the other hand, was so laid back he was almost comatose. He'd retired a detective, the benefits had been great and the two shots he'd taken to the chest hadn't hurt his settlement upon leaving the department as an injured cop. He was delighted his daughter had Vargas blood, as opposed to a trailer trash princess mentality, as he called it, that she had grit and the desire to give something back to the community.

"Nah," she'd told him when he'd bragged on her once, "I just like that conceal and carry permit and the license to beat the crap out of men who piss me off."

She'd still been in the academy when he took his retirement bullets, as he called the shots that almost felled him. She'd gone to his hospital bedside, run errands and somehow managed to soften the old codger, who took to inviting her over for the occasional poker tournament with his retired buddies or to watch his team, the Texas Longhorns, play football.

Charlie wasn't stupid. She knew that fifty percent, if not more, of his sudden interest in his daughter once she was out of high school and college, was that he wanted to keep tabs on her. He had friends in every nook and cranny of government and law enforcement across the state who watched her and reported back to him. Maybe it was because he had such a strained relationship with her mother that he wasn't more forthcoming and didn't simply ask her how she was or what she'd been doing. Hell, maybe he just didn't trust that she was capable of looking after herself. Not like he didn't know the dangers young women faced, much less female cops.

Didn't matter to Charlie. She was glad to finally have a father and to see a side of him her mother had either ignored or failed to mention, that of a dad who gave a damn. And whenever Charlie had a particularly hard case or needed advice, she went to Sam, who was a good listener.

In typical Sam fashion, he had a pot of cheese dip simmering in a Crock-Pot and a batch of her favorite cookies, chocolate chip, cooling on the stove when she walked in the door carrying the beer.

"Set it in the refrigerator, kid. I cleared a space," he instructed, stirring his cheese dip. "I'll give you a kiss in a sec. Oh, and turn down the television. I've seen that episode before, and it sucks. Besides, you sounded depressed. What's up?"

She hauled the beer out of the sack and popped open two cans, taking one over to him and tilting her cheek for the kiss.

"Remember that guy I was seeing last year, the one who disappeared?"

"Yep. This has something to do with him?" Sam asked, quirking an eyebrow. "I thought you said you were over him."

"I lied. And I think he's back, but I'm not sure." She explained the situation.

Sam whistled and sat across the small kitchen island from her. "Pass me the salsa. So what do you think? Is it him?"

"I don't know." She shrugged.

"Bullshit. You been to bed with him yet?"

"Daddy!" Charlie lapsed from adult cop to that of shocked child.

"What? An old man can't ask his daughter if she's getting any?"

"No, you may not. And the answer is no, not that it's any of your business."

"Hey, a father has rights." He munched the chips and swigged his beer. "You know, there was something funny about the way you said he left, so maybe this guy's the real deal, and maybe there's nothing more to it than he got a bad bump on the head—okay, and a facelift—in Mexico." Sam crossed his arms over his chest. "Bring him around here. Let me have a look at him."

"I will not. Not yet, anyway."

"Ah, so there is something going on between the two of you."

"He kissed me, okay?" Charlie felt herself blush. "It was just a kiss, but…it… It felt like him, you know? There was something there besides hormones and testosterone and all that icky, touchy-feely stuff."

"God, you sound like me now. Careful. I'm already in enough trouble with your mother. You cheat her out of a church wedding, should this man be the one, and she'll put out a contract on me."

"If Mom planned a wedding, not that there is anything remotely like that going on between us, it'd be held in a bingo parlor, and you know it." Charlie sipped her beer. "Tell her I said so, though, and you die for sure."

"Okay, Charlene, what's this really about?" Sam indicated the beer. "You bring a six-pack when you just want to say hi and a twelve-pack when you're troubled, and there's at least a case in my refrigerator, thanks to you. So what's the problem? He's back—so what? He doesn't remember you, or you don't remember him, or what?"

"I think it's him, but we can't prove it. I've run AFIS, you name it, and the man either doesn't exist except in my imagination, or he's a Fed."

"Or he's more than that," Sam said. "Maybe he's not even American."

"No, he's ours."

"How do you know? What are the facts, not the feelings? Time for that later." Sam propped his head in his palms, rubbing his lower lip with a thumb. Ready to brainstorm.

"He has no distinguishing marks, scars or features—he's just a nice-looking man who could be anybody. He doesn't have an accent."

"Again, that could be a cover."

Charlie nodded. "He doesn't have a driver's license, which raises a red flag."

"Big one if he's Texan," Sam said. "So maybe he's from the East Coast and is used to walking everywhere, or maybe the friggin' cab drivers in this town make him as nuts as they do the rest of us."

Charlie shook her head. "It's more than that. He's familiar with Houston. He's just not familiar with himself, who he is, and I get the feeling he's afraid of driving for some reason, now that I think back. Maybe it's because of the accident now, but…weird, isn't it, that he didn't drive before then?"

Sam shrugged. "Hell, lots of people don't get their driver's licenses, but most of those folks are from a big city. Houston is huge, has been for over a decade, but it's too spread out for a walker unless he sticks to one particular neighborhood, so he's either not from here, or he has a girlfriend." He seemed to catch himself. "Sorry. Or somebody."

"Thanks, Sam." Charlie knew her voice dripped sarcasm.

"Welcome. It's what I do best. Stick my foot in my mouth."

"No, maybe you're right. Maybe he has a girlfriend." She hated to admit it, but at this point, truth was more important than ego.

Her father pushed himself away from the island. "Grab a bowl of chips, fill another with dip and grab a notebook and pen. We'll come up with something. We're two smart people." He chuckled. "Can't say the same for the Aldridge woman and her husband. Who in their right mind tries convincing someone they are somebody else?"

"Folks who don't have to worry about anyone contradicting them." Charlie chewed her bottom lip a moment. "If Mason Aldridge was a bit of a hermit, rarely went into his office, didn't socialize, it'd be conceivable."

While he hauled out utensils and dishes, he hummed, and Charlie felt more at ease than she had all day. Then again, she argued with herself, maybe she was just tired and hungry.

Then Sam turned, holding the dipper for the cheese as if he were directing an orchestra, punctuating his sentences with every syllable. "You know. Maybe we're looking at this all wrong. Think back to when he first entered your life. What were you working on?"

"I don't get what that has to do with anything." Charlie frowned.

"Maybe his accident had nothing to do with him

and more to do with you. That's all." He paused, waiting for her to comment again.

Charlie considered what he'd said but shook her head. "Don't think so. I was working on the Martin case, man who'd been dead for six weeks or so, and one of his old girlfriends came by to say she thought he'd been murdered."

"Where did Martin live?"

"Downtown. Some hotel."

"Must be nice. What'd he do to earn his money?"

"He worked at an escort service. We never could pin them down. They had a massive operation with several hundred employees, but none of the execs were ever in town, and…" She stopped, staring straight ahead. "Last time Martin was seen was before he boarded a plane for Mexico."

She looked at her dad then cocked her head, her frown deepening. "Seth, an escort? I don't see it."

"Hey, I'm only askin' you to consider it. Dig back and see what you were doing. An escort wouldn't be required to drive. A courier would, just about anyone else would, but an escort would go where he was taken."

Charlie suddenly felt as if she was the one who'd been taken. By a gigolo or a charlatan or just a snake who might have been between girlfriends when he'd romanced her. "I really hate it when you do that."

"What's that?"

"Play devil's advocate and wind up making me doubt what I feel is a solid lead."

Sam chuckled. "I wasn't aware you had any."

"You know what really ticks me off?" Charlie stifled the gall she felt growing, the bitter taste in her mouth. "I can't even get angry with him. He doesn't remember a damn thing."

"Kinda steals your thunder, doesn't it?" Sam smiled ruefully.

Charlie had a thought. "Okay if I borrow your laptop? Heather was supposed to send me a photo or two of a car, maybe of the men watching us at the restaurant today."

"Sure—help yourself. You know where it is. Bring it in here, though," her dad said. "Not that I don't trust you and me, what with our savvy and quick minds and all, but doesn't hurt to have a good search engine when you're brainstorming."

Charlie's cell phone rang before she could retrieve the laptop, and she looked at the number. Last time he'd called, she'd plugged in one word. Seth. She pressed the button, answering his call. "Yes?"

She saw her dad watching her and turned her back, more out of fear she'd blush than concern he'd overhear her conversation.

"Would you be willing to fly south with me tomorrow?"

"We talking birds, geese-type flying to South America, or what?" she asked, looking for a lighter avenue in tone so she could calm her jangled nerves.

"Mexico. Guadalajara is where the accident occurred. I'd like to speak with the doctors who treated me—face to face this time instead of over the phone."

Charlie was surprised. "Sure. I'd have to clear it with my captain tomorrow."

"I'll ring you around eight. That too soon?"

"No, it's fine. I'll talk to you then and let you know what he says."

Charlie turned back to face her father after she hung up. "You'll never guess…"

"Yes, I would," he cut in. "It was him. Otherwise, you wouldn't have turned away like that."

She set her jaw and smirked. "Could you stop being a cop for just five seconds?"

"Could you?"

"Probably not. Yes, it was Seth. He wants me to fly to Mexico with him tomorrow."

"Pack an umbrella," Sam said nonchalantly, as if she'd just suggested they go to lunch. "They've got some storms moving in from the Caribbean. Saw that on the news yesterday. Wouldn't want anything to put a damper on things for you."

When she remained where she was, Sam cleared his throat. "Forget something?"

"Hmm?"

Her dad smiled indulgently. "Now I know some of what I must've missed when you were a starry-eyed teenager with her first crush." He cocked his head toward the back of his house. "You were supposed to get my laptop and bring it in here so we could do some searching online."

"Oh. Yeah." Jeez. She'd all but forgotten that she also needed to look for Heather's email containing snapshots of the men who were following her and Seth.

CHAPTER FOUR

CHARLIE AND SAM HAD STAYED UP so late going over what little evidence she had that indicated Seth was possibly a Fed that she'd decided to spend the night on her dad's couch. Not like she hadn't done so before, but she had to scurry home the next morning for a shower and change of clothes.

Seth's plan had made sense—fly to Mexico and interview the sources. Perhaps the doctors who had given him his new face would have information regarding his condition when he'd come in, specifics on circumstances when the paperwork for the surgeries had been signed, all of the details he hadn't been able to secure on his own once he was back in Houston. With Charlie flashing a badge, maybe they'd get somewhere.

When she agreed, Seth booked them on the quickest flight out of Houston for late morning. All Charlie had to do was square things with her boss, let her captain know she was trying to tie Seth's disappearance to a cold case that had crossed her desk earlier and reiterate the fact that the department wouldn't need to pick up the tab, not even her lunch, considering "Mason Aldridge" was paying for everything.

"Might as well let the old boy foot the bill, considering we'll be investigating his disappearance as well while we're there," Seth had said.

Captain Bemo told Charlie to let her new partner know and to take the rest of the day off. "It's Wednesday," he said. "Think you can find out what you need to know and be back here by Monday?"

Charlie had jumped at the chance.

She requested George Martin's file be copied and put on a thumb drive so she could study it on the plane, but before she left, the clerk who'd taken the information called her back into the room.

"What's wrong, Julie?" Charlie asked.

"Just thought you'd like to know. Lots of activity on this file," Julie said. She looked over the top of her glasses at Charlie and blinked. "Three days ago, your new partner. Last month, the CIA, no less."

"You sure?" Concerned, Charlie rounded the corner to peer over Julie's shoulder. "Wonder why?"

Julie wrote down a code and handed it to her. "Whoever it was must think Martin links to one of their cases. Who knows?"

Charlie glanced at the note. The date Julie had written beside the agent's inquiry code was only two weeks prior. First the Feds were tailing Seth—now this. "What the devil?" she mused, sticking the note into her jacket pocket. She'd have to ask Bemo about it when she got back from Mexico.

Mexico. She stopped midway up a flight of steps, thinking. She'd never been as far south as Guadalajara, but she'd bet it was beautiful and that with the right swimsuit and any luck, even in March she could get a tan.

Silly, she chided herself. *You're not going there to swim or sunbathe. Besides, Sam told you to expect storms.* She continued up the steps, irked that she'd even thought of such a thing. She knew she looked pretty good. Better than average. The thought of dressing in a skimpy bikini and possibly rattling Seth's memory cells a bit was tantalizing, but her appearance was probably the farthest thing from the man's mind.

She felt one corner of her lips lift as she continued the sparring match her femininity had going with her logic. Just because they weren't going to the beach didn't mean she couldn't dress differently than she did at work. Pack a sundress or two, some strappy sandals and a light, cashmere sweater for the March nights. The area's rainy season would be starting within a few weeks, but reports were that storms in the Caribbean were already causing inland problems.

"You look like la gata, the proverbial cat that swallowed the bird."

She lifted her head as she heard Rodríguez coming down the steps to halt beside her. She smiled in greeting. "Hey. I was just coming to see you."

"Bemo phoned me to tell me. Said you looked like your head was in the clouds, so he wasn't sure if you'd get hold of me or not." Rodríguez grinned and pulled down the shades that he wore even inside the building. "Hot date?"

"If you talked to Bemo, then you know the answer."

"Yah, but it was the quickest way I could think of to break the ice. You're always so reserved." He winked. "Can I come?"

"I don't think there's room for you in my luggage, Rodríguez, but nice try."

He dropped into step beside her as she turned to return to the floor she'd just left. "Hey, you might need an interpreter."

She stopped and looked at him. "Now that is not a bad idea."

"Just sayin', call me if you get into trouble. I still speak the lingo." He was suddenly serious, the smooth naturally tanned face no longer smiling. "I opened George Martin's file. Nasty way to die. The guy carved him up like a Thanksgiving turkey."

"Yeah." Just thinking of the gruesome murder gave Charlie chills. "Why are you poking around in there?"

"You're my partner, it's one of the cases you've worked on for several months and it's one of the few you haven't solved. Thought perhaps you could use some fresh eyes on it."

She chucked him on the arm with a light tap of her fist. "Thanks. We'll do that together when I get back. Deal?" She held out her hand for him to shake.

She hid a smile as his face broke into a wide,

warm grin. She could tell he was thrilled she'd finally accepted that he might be the guy who had her back in a fight.

"You got it," he said.

"Oh, and Julio?"

"Yeah?"

"A friend is supposed to send me some candid shots she took with her camera phone. A couple of guys were following me yesterday. Well, maybe not just me. Anyway, when I get them, okay if I forward them to you if she got the tag so you can run it for me?"

Now his chest swelled. She chuckled. The guy was growing on her. Maybe he wouldn't make such a bad partner after all.

Seth was waiting for her at the airport, cups of coffee from a specialty shop in each hand. It was his attire that intrigued her, though, and the sight of him in the jeans and a nice pullover sweater made her heart skip a beat.

He waited for her to clear the checkpoint and sat beside her while she slipped her shoes back on.

Charlie was glad she'd taken a tip from Rodríguez and worn dark glasses. The shades hid her expression, so she knew Seth couldn't see that she watched him assess her figure. She knew she looked good in the outfit she'd chosen, a soft pink bolero tee paired with heather-gray slacks and matching jacket. The only flair items she added were a pair of black pumps with coordinating shoulder bag and trench coat, should she need it.

"You look nice," he said, giving a brief nod of his head.

Charlie hoped she wasn't beaming as she thanked him. "I was going for a look that said 'I'm not really a cop but don't mess with me.'"

"Don't think you'll have to worry about that," he said, his voice hinting of laughter. When she puckered her forehead with a perplexed frown, he indicated the holster and Glock 30 strapped across her chest beneath the jacket she'd put back on once she was out of the line.

Charlie laughed. "Well, I suppose that helps boost my tough-chick meter up a notch or two. Can't get on the plane without showing it, and I'm not getting off the plane without having it on my person."

"Sure." He walked beside her down the hall to their gate. "Thought maybe you could use the coffee," he said. "We have about a thirty-minute wait before we board."

"Oh, yes." She accepted the drink. "Thanks. I didn't have time for breakfast this morning, and I'm not a happy camper without my caffeine."

"Want something to eat?" he asked. "We have time."

She shook her head. "Can't fly with food in my stomach, but thanks anyway. Maybe when we arrive. Can you recommend any place once we're there? I've never been to the coast."

He looked as if he was about to say something then changed his mind. Finally, he quit walking. "You know, that question off the cuff like that... I started to say the name of a restaurant, and my mind went blank. But for a moment...for just a brief instant, it was there." He blinked. "Wonder what that means."

Charlie took a deep breath. "I don't know squat about head injuries, but my dad and I discussed your situation last night at his place, and he thinks you could fully recover your memory in time. I told him what you'd told me, and he said he's heard of cases where one day the information just starts flowing, like a jammed fountain that's been unclogged. Not everything at once, but in pieces."

Seth seemed to be processing the information. It was difficult to tell from his expression what he was thinking, but his eyes held a strange sense of peace, and Charlie sincerely hoped that no matter what happened between the two of them, he'd recover fully. He had to be in hell not knowing anything about his past. Seemed like it'd make everything in the present all the more difficult to handle, from what to do, to who to trust, to whether or not he could even manage a task set before him.

"There's something I've been meaning to ask," she said once they found their gate and took two seats facing the runways. "You phoned the doctors, right, to let them know we were coming? What did they say?"

Seth stretched his legs, crossing them at the ankles. "One doctor said no problem—he even offered to copy the records for me. The plastic surgeon, on the other hand, was a tough nut to crack. I got the feeling he was withholding information, like he was afraid I'd sue him or something. Not sure what's up with that." Seth shrugged. "I'm sure I'm more than a little paranoid since this happened, though, so I'll give him the benefit of the doubt until we meet him."

Charlie furrowed her brow. "Paranoid?"

He shrugged. "Always suspecting someone's motives, never quite understanding what my relationship is to them if we're supposed to be friends or family."

"Has your supposed sister offered any ideas, or did you talk to her?" Charlie asked. "I would think she'd have plenty to say."

"You'd be wrong. She and I don't talk. One of the reasons I made sure she wasn't on any of my personal financial accounts and why I moved out of the house last night is because I don't trust her."

Charlie held up a hand. "Wait. You moved—out of the mansion?"

"Into the Hyatt on Louisiana. She hasn't said or done anything that indicates she had a bad relationship with her brother, but once we figured out I wasn't Mason Aldridge, I realized he has to be dead." He chuckled. "I'm not afraid of her killing me in my sleep or anything. It just creeped me out thinking that the guy I replaced had to be dead and that she must know something about it if she's willing to perjure herself by claiming I'm her brother. And if we prove beyond doubt that I'm not Mason, this will wind up in court. She has to know this."

"Yeah." Charlie set her jaw. "Sam and I talked about that last night, too."

"Sam?"

"My dad. I know it's probably strange to hear me call him by his first name, but our relationship is weird. I didn't get to know him very well until I graduated the academy. He and my mom fought like cats, so he was never around when I was a kid."

"Do you know anything more about—that is…if I'm Seth…" He paused and looked at her thoughtfully. "One of the worst things about all of this is that I don't know one way or the other."

"I know." She gathered courage for something else she'd meant to ask him. "Why don't we assume…for now…that you are Seth? At least you'd have a name, and I wouldn't be calling you John Doe or anything inane like that."

He nodded. "That works for me. I've already started keeping track of every dime I'm spending of Aldridge money. Once I figure out just who I am, my former job, all of it—I intend to pay every cent back to the Aldridge Foundation. The business, Aldridge Manufacturing, is owned by the foundation as a whole. That's who deposits money into my account every month." He shrugged. "I know—

they're robbing me of my identity, and I should be suing them, but while I'm figuring all of this out, I'm living in a not-too-shabby home, eating expensive meals and dressing rather well." He looked down at his pants. "I've even been shopping. I figure if it's her money, that's one thing. But if I'm spending Mason's money—he didn't do this to me. No need to take advantage of him."

"So you're booked on the flights as Aldridge." She didn't know why she hadn't thought of that, but it made sense. He had no identification, no way to fly without some form of it.

"You disapprove?" he asked.

Charlie lifted her hands. "Hey, whatever works. It's not my money, and you're not breaking any laws that I know of, so have at it, but what happens if the real Aldridge appears, just shows up some day?"

Seth snorted. "Then I guess I'll owe him a big apology for helping drain his accounts, or he'll owe me one for saddling me with his sister. Hell, he may not be missing at all—the man might be hiding. If you had to live with Dorinda and Doug, you'd understand."

Charlie listened as he spoke, to the deep timbre of his voice, noticing the absence of inflections that might have told her something about his background. Normally, people had accents, and she was good at identifying them to within close proximity of where they'd grown up. With Seth, she was baffled.

While he appeared more at ease with her today,

he was still aloof, certainly not impolite or rude, but definitely more reserved than she'd have preferred. They were a nice-looking couple, if she did think so, and traveling to one of the hottest Mexican Riviera locales on the map. It would've been nice if they could've truly been a couple, her arm linked through his, his eyes maintaining with hers a steady communication of mutual respect and admiration, if not love.

She seemed to be the farthest thing from her companion's mind, though. He talked about where he'd booked their hotel, how long 'til they arrived, and the fact that he was even talking to her made her smile. She and Seth had talked before, but she hadn't realized until this moment how much she'd missed hearing his voice.

I shouldn't have worn this get-up. She glanced down at her nice, crisp suit, halfheartedly listening to him now. She should have donned her usual uniform of military-pressed pants, sturdy walking shoes and a button-down shirt. They were to interview a coroner and a couple of doctors, not sip margaritas poolside and stroll hand in hand through downtown Guadalajara. She felt like a fool for wanting...and expecting...to jar his memory, to have him snap out of whatever was keeping him from remembering his past, from remembering her.

Charlie hadn't played with dolls as a little girl—she'd played with pen and paper, she'd collected dead bugs and examined spiderwebs. She'd loved to solve puzzles and play hide-and-seek, and her favorite game had been Clue, primarily because it dealt with facts instead of emotions.

Her mother had seen to it that Charlie grew up knowing how to dress and wear makeup, walk in heels and deal with bad hair days. June's biggest lesson she'd taught her daughter, however, had been to know when a boy was lying to her by watching his eyes and hands. None of it had prepared Charlie for dating life, but it had served her well as a cop.

Sam's teachings, once she'd reached adulthood, had been to show Charlie how to hold a rifle, to do a roundhouse kick and knock a man out with the heel of her foot, and to swim safely in the shark-infested waters off the Gulf. Nobody had bothered with nonsensical things like helping her feel comfortable flirting, so Charlie was a complete dodo bird when it came to feminine wiles unless she was witnessing another woman use them on some unsuspecting man at the precinct.

"Have you heard anything I've said the past five minutes?" Seth asked, giving her an amused smile.

"Yes, sorry. I'm listening. You said you'd booked us a suite on the outskirts of the city, but I didn't catch why so far away."

Seth folded his arms. "You were probably the kid who could sleep during class with her eyes open, too, weren't you? Because that was a lucky guess."

"It's not a guess if I'm on the same page with you," she said, feeling self-conscious. Had she been lucky, or was he letting her believe she wasn't a dumbstruck fool every time she looked at him?

Charlie gave him a direct stare. "Okay, I'll admit it—I've missed hearing your voice. You used to do this a lot...before, you know? We could discuss anything from the weather to world hunger, and you'd have an opinion or know something to add that I hadn't thought about, and I..." She shrugged. "I've missed it."

He grinned. "I don't remember much, but I know what I like when I see it, and I'm pretty sure I've always appreciated candor and honesty. You aren't the type to hide what you're feeling, are you?"

"I'd like to be," she admitted ruefully. "I'm just not very good at playing head games."

"Good." He took a deep breath, one that seemed to extend from his nostrils to his toes, because he flexed as he inhaled, very slowly, and he closed his eyes.

Charlie wondered what he was thinking, but she wasn't ready to get quite that personal with him. While she longed to feel his arms about her again, this man was someone she didn't quite know, probably because he didn't know himself. It would be too much like seducing him while he was still comatose not to give him the chance to remember things on his own.

An airline employee announced their flight. She and Seth gathered their single pieces of luggage and walked toward the ramp leading into their plane.

Charlie shivered as a creepy thought snuck into her brain. Guadalajara might be an upscale resort area, much different from many rural areas of the country, but it was still foreign territory, with different laws and ways of enforcing them. She prayed she and Seth wouldn't run afoul of anything that would prohibit them from reentering the country. While she was certain she knew the man at her side before his accident, she didn't know that much about him. What if he was in trouble with the law in Mexico?

She handed her ticket to the flight attendant and waited while he returned the stub. What if this new Seth caused her an endless amount of grief that had nothing to do with her heart? Was any part of her safe with him?

THE AIRPORT IN Guadalajara seemed small for serving a city of five million, with only two terminals, one for international flights, the other for domestic. It was a one-story structure, with an almost all-glass front. Charlie was happy to see a Starbucks almost as soon as they'd disembarked.

Customs was a red-light, green-light affair once they received their luggage, and the lines moved quickly, especially considering the traffic the minute airport handled.

Seth spotted their driver with the sign bearing the Aldridge name, and soon he and Charlie were speeding through the city for their hotel. Dozens of trees lined the boulevards and side streets, and there was an odd smell, much like that of a mild eucalyptus, that tickled Charlie's nostrils.

As they drove past downtown, other scents permeated the air. Street foods—tamales and tacos, the smells of fried pork, cabbage, peppers and salsa. The midday bustle and hustle was energizing, even after their hour-or-so flight.

As for their hotel, Seth had chosen well. Their posh palace north of the city was perfect, with landscaping that would have done any hotelier or private landowner proud, and two adjoining suites that shared an open kitchen, dining area, living room and balcony overlooking the expansive lawns. Each bedroom had a private bath with a sunken spa tub, and plush towels and washcloths.

Once they'd checked in and unpacked, Seth suggested they use the car and driver he'd hired to take them into Guadalajara to scope out where they needed to go and to find a good restaurant since Charlie hadn't eaten in several hours.

"What if the doctors and medical examiner won't see us?" she asked again, not remembering what he'd said earlier. Her head was already swimming with information. She'd blame it on jet lag, but the flight had only been a little over an hour.

"We go south to the U.S. Embassy in Mexico City." Seth held up his hands. "I know. It's nearly three hundred miles and would entail several hours driving, but maybe we won't have to go there." He chuckled at her frown. "Don't worry—maybe the trip won't be necessary"

"I hope not." Charlie stewed on the new information. "There's no way my boss will let me go for the extra time."

"Agree. The swine flu outbreak during the past two years has been horrid on travel here," he told her. "Shame, really, because Mexico is a beautiful country."

She wondered how much he remembered and how much he'd simply read since his accident. "Don't take this the wrong way, but aren't you curious about where the accident occurred?"

He nodded. "I've even asked if the driver we hired can take us there long enough for me to walk around. Thought perhaps it'd jog my memory." He smiled sadly. "If nothing else, maybe it'll give me an idea of how bad the accident was. I never did see photos of either car. All I know is that I woke up with a face I don't recognize. I'd like to see if these surgeries were necessary."

Charlie grimaced. "That's pretty diabolical, that the Aldridges would have your face changed to suit their own purposes."

"Maybe it's paranoia talking, and maybe it's common sense," he responded. "I mean, who would have benefited by my death and who would benefit by my living? Why did my face have to change? Was it really that badly mangled, or did Dorinda simply need a brother to show up in the States when she returned?"

Charlie assumed Dorinda must've loved her brother, at least a little. But she couldn't help but wonder at the gall it had taken to work up such an elaborate scheme to make Seth believe he was Mason. Either Dorinda needed a physical brother for whatever reasons, and the Feds needed a plant in the Aldridge midst, even if he was unaware at the time. Or they all were losing IQ points every time they took a leak. None of it made sense, but if it kept Seth alive, it was worth checking into as far as Charlie was concerned.

Seth walked from the living area to stare out the French doors leading to the balcony. He opened them and inhaled deeply as he walked onto the landing, lifting his head toward the sun. Charlie strolled out to stand beside him and look onto the mountains below.

Water burbled from carved stone fountains that dotted the statue-studded grounds, and vivid flowers swayed in the slight breeze along well-appointed borders and trimmed hedges. A pink-bricked esplanade wound from their perch atop one mountain to the valley and beach below then upward toward yet another hilly area that looked to be part of the same establishment.

Surrounding their hotel were rugged cliffs and giant monoliths that Charlie could easily believe had been around since the beginning of time. Fifteenth and sixteenth century structures, probably churches, in the distance added to the charm and seclusion of the area.

The weather was sunny, but the humidity was palpable, and clouds were rolling in from the west and south. Sam might have been correct because Charlie sensed a storm brewing. Guadalajara wasn't as warm and sunny as La Paz, and it wasn't that much warmer than Mexico City, but it was right off the ocean and whatever storms that might blow in from the western Caribbean.

She looked at Seth's face. His eyes were dark, brooding. It was as if he searched the hills for answers to something that troubled him.

Of course. She touched his arm. "Where specifically did the accident happen?"

He swallowed, hard, and he shook his head slowly, not as if he was dismissing her but as if the subject was too painful. She followed his gaze…and knew. It had happened here or close. He'd chosen their hotel for a reason.

Hadn't he mentioned that he'd secured the accident report? The location of the wreck would have been on it. Maybe not a detailed description, or enough of one to lend many clues, but he'd have been given pertinent information to at least get him in the vicinity, even if he didn't know precisely where it had occurred.

"I don't know where I was staying prior," he said, "but the wreck was on the highway we took to get here. We passed it, I'm sure. I watched the car's odometer and calculated the miles as we drove. My hope is that we can have someone take us there. Maybe a police officer."

"Good idea." She didn't know what else to say. She'd have done the same if it had been her who had nearly lost her life. She'd want to know, especially if she had no recollection of what had happened.

"Do you want to follow up on where that woman was staying?" she asked. "The one who hit you?"

"Yes, if you don't mind."

"Not at all."

The scent of rain drifted around them, and soon lightning flashed in the distance.

"We'd better head for town if you're ready," he said, turning to walk inside and placing a hand on the small of her back to guide her.

Charlie knew he was right, but she wanted to ask him one more question as soon as they were safely inside. "What's it like, the memory loss?"

Seth thought a moment. "At first, there were the headaches, residual physical problems that come with any type of healing. What was worse was feeling out of control, not knowing who to trust, what exactly had happened or was happening. I didn't know Dorinda or her husband, Doug. I didn't recognize the house once we were back in Houston. There wasn't much I could do."

"And the other problems?" Charlie prompted.

"Paranoia," he said with a small, sad laugh.

"Missing pieces of a puzzle and not knowing what the entire picture was supposed to look like, just knowing there were parts that belonged that weren't there. Agoraphobia—I was afraid to leave the mansion for several weeks. I had a driver, a butler, two men who for some reason I trusted, even though they looked at me like I was some creature from outer space.

"Even my damned clothes bothered me." Then he laughed, this time with real humor lacing the sound. "The night before I met with you, I had a bit of a tantrum, for lack of a better word, smack in the middle of my clothes closet. I couldn't find anything to wear in a room that held probably three dozen suits, twice as many shirts and innumerable pairs of shoes. I flopped onto my back on the floor and stared at the ceiling, trying to get a handle on what bothered me, and I realized I had no jeans. Of all the crazy things. Pretty lame, huh?"

Charlie grinned. "Not really. You—that is, when I knew you, that was what you wore most of the time. Levi's 501, button down. You had the best butt in those."

Why on earth would you say that, Charlie? She was immediately self-conscious.

Seth took her arm and steered her toward her shoulder bag on the dining room table. "Let's go before I grab you and thank you properly for that compliment."

CHAPTER FIVE

THE DRIVE INTO GUADALAJARA was short, but the winding road definitely triggered all manner of responses from Seth. He tried to relax, to trust the driver with directions, to trust himself sitting close to Charlie. Her casual words at the hotel had instantly put him at ease while also making him realize how standoffish he must seem. What she must be going through, being so close physically yet at the same time so far removed from a former lover who couldn't recall anything of what they'd shared.

And he knew instinctively that they had been lovers. He could sense it in the way he caught her looking at him, warily yet longingly. Seth wanted to reassure her that it would all come back to him, but there were no guarantees.

Most of his mistrust lay within himself, not for the hope of the brain's power to heal itself, but for his heart not to override his cognitive process. He couldn't afford to get swept away in a relationship with Charlie until he knew who he was, how he was capable of dealing with things, with himself, his situation, his family...if he had one. How to manage the one he supposedly had, when he knew they were lying to him, that he wasn't truly an Aldridge.

Now and then he'd get flashes that had to be memory, but the scenes and still shots in his mind were random, and they made no sense. Him holding a gun, pointing it at someone or something just beyond the mental boundaries his mind constructed. Marjorie Lawson's face, as if he knew her prior to the wreck, which was ludicrous unless they were in the same car...and the reports said otherwise.

None of it made sense. If he had memories of any woman, wouldn't they be of Charlie?

She stirred next to him, crossing her legs as she leaned toward her side of the car, peering out her window. He looked at her profile, feeling a stirring in his groin. He didn't remember being with her before, but he sure wanted her now. If they hadn't been traveling toward information to clarify his past, he'd have worked on their present relationship, what little there was. She was lovely. Small but willowy, with short blond hair, amazing brown eyes and a pert confidence. Deceptive, he was certain, because he'd sensed a well-hidden vulnerability when he'd kissed her at the police station.

Now her face was serene, and for all their driver knew, she could be a woman touring his country, taking in the wild countryside now, and later the bustling city with its centuries of history and perfect blend of modern technology and old-world charm.

Charlie may have been the one wearing a gun,

but Seth felt a strange protectiveness toward her, and not because of her stature. Dynamite indeed came in small packages, and he had no doubts that the spitfire beside him could handle herself in any situation, but he wanted to guard her, have her back, be with her.

"You are staring at me." Her voice was quiet, calm, with a hint of amusement. She hadn't turned to look at him, but continued looking out her window.

"Yes. I'm sorry." Seth felt flustered. "I'm trying to remember...things."

Charlie nodded. "Time for that later. Concentrate on what you'll say to the doctors and the medical examiner, if we can find him." Then she did look directly at him. "Assuming you wish to know more about Marjorie Lawson."

Again, he nodded. "I figured with your credentials, you could gain an audience with him easier than I could.'

"You'd be correct. Just don't expect much. He'll be reluctant to say anything, and he'll most likely notify the police as soon as we've left. They don't like our government interfering with their work."

"Understandable." He accepted her assessment, knowing she was right. He'd be lucky if the doctors gave more than cursory comments echoing whatever was written on their reports. Not like they'd have American car crash victims every day, but their workload had to be horrendous in such a busy area of Mexico. They might not even remember him.

Soon their driver stopped outside the glass doors of the hospital, and Seth and Charlie exited the car. Signs were primarily in Spanish, but they soon located a hospital directory and the elevators. Seth pressed the correct buttons to take them to their floor.

A clock on the wall at the nurse's station indicated the hour, still early afternoon, but if their hospital shifts were anything like those of their American counterparts, the staff would soon switch, so they had to work quickly.

Dr. Juan Murrieta was still a resident, and he was making final rounds before his shift ended. One of the nurses ushered them to a waiting area on the floor and told them to wait, that she would send him in as soon as he turned in his reports. Seth hated waiting, but he did as she suggested. Charlie, however, made excuses to go to the ladies' room. Something about her voice suggested to Seth that she had plans to do more than visit the lavatory. He watched as she strode confidently back to the nurses' station and motioned for one of the nurses to speak with her.

What is it about women, he wondered, *that they could draw a stone into a conversation?* Many of them were chatterboxes who needed an audience or to share information. Men, he'd noted, were nothing like that. Men said their piece and moved on. They went to stores, purchased what was necessary, then left. Women…could talk and mingle and chat for hours. Charlie hadn't struck him as talkative, but it was obvious she was good at getting others to trust her because the nurse she'd beckoned hadn't stopped talking since being called over.

Soon Charlie, the nurse and a short, spectacled man in hospital fatigues moved toward Seth. Once they stood before him, the man in hospital whites held out his hand and introduced himself as Dr. Murrieta, the resident on duty the night Seth had come into the hospital.

"Dr. Murrieta says you were brought in by ambulance," Charlie told Seth, "but the nurse—this is Mercedes Gómez—was on duty that night, and she says two police officers had you in the back of their car, that they were patrolling the area that night and saw the vehicle that slammed into both your car and that of Ms. Lawson."

"Sí," Gómez interjected. "It was raining that night, and there were other accidents. No ambulance available until much later to drive to the cliffs." She lowered her head when Murrieta cut her a sharp look. "No disrespect, Doctor, but you were very busy that night. I know the policemen who brought this man inside."

When it looked as if the nurse wasn't challenging him, merely correcting a misconception, the doctor's face brightened into what looked like a false smile. He nodded. "Yes, I was very busy, as I am now." He glanced at his watch in an obvious attempt to get rid of them.

"What about the other doctors who worked on

me?" Seth asked, afraid Murrieta would leave before divulging any more information.

"You had severe head trauma, and we did not know if you would live. Once you were stable, I saw your condition and recommended reconstruction, of course," Murrieta said. "We are a small hospital, but we have a fine plastic surgeon on staff."

Seth took the opportunity, before Murrieta could leave, to ask yet another question, this time about his medical records, of which the doctor claimed no knowledge. "You'll need to speak with someone downstairs who handles that sort of thing," he said.

As if on cue, Charlie touched the doctor's arm gently. "Would you be a gentleman and show me the way?" she asked. "I'll walk with you."

"What of Señor Aldridge?" asked the doctor, who all but sputtered. He obviously didn't like being tag-teamed by the Americans.

"I believe he has other questions for your nurse. He'll meet us in a few minutes." Charlie smiled pleasantly, but Seth could see irritation rising in Murrieta's face and mirth in the nurse's. Murrieta glanced down at his arm, leaving no doubt as to his displeasure that the foreign law enforcement officer had dared touch him, even briefly.

Mercedes Gómez turned her head and coughed gently to hide her laughter, and Seth held out a hand to her, taking Charlie's lead.

"While Detective Vargas walks with the doctor, do you think you could direct me to the coroner's lab?" he asked of her, emphasizing Charlie's title for the doctor's benefit, in case he thought he'd dodge the request without hassle. "I'm afraid my Spanish isn't so good, and many of your signs are only in your language. I apologize for the inconvenience."

Her eyes met his in silent acknowledgement, and she led him in the opposite direction.

Charlie called over her shoulder that she'd find him and meet him in medical records since he'd have to sign for them.

Once they were out of earshot of Murrieta, Gómez stopped and faced Seth, her dark eyes troubled. "You should know something." She looked about nervously before continuing. "Dr. Murrieta was not the one who suggested the plastic surgery you had. Your sister did. What Dr. Murrieta recommended was reconstructive surgery that didn't require breaking your jawbone and realigning it, but your sister insisted."

Seth was shocked. "She wanted my face reshaped?"

At Seth's puzzled frown, she proceeded, her head and voice low, obviously so as not to cause distraction. "Dr. Murrieta didn't even know you had a sister until she came to him. There was a storm, and we had many accidents that night, so the hospital was full. I saw her outside your room one night, and she was reading your chart. Then she slammed shut the folder, grabbed the man with her—her husband I believe—and told him they needed to talk." Gómez shrugged. "The next day she approached Dr. Murrieta. Within two days a doctor in California flew down here, and he was assisted by Dr. Martínez, who has a small clinic for those who can't afford medical attention."

"What do you mean?" Seth asked. "My sister... California... I don't understand. How long after the accident before my...before she read my chart?"

"Maybe a week? She'd been here about that long and was to be released the next day." The nurse gave him a don't-you-remember-anything? look. "Three cars involved, with you, your sister and your brother-in-law supposedly in one car."

"Supposedly?" Seth felt stupid for echoing her and asking so many questions.

The nurse shrugged. "So she says. My brother is a police officer. I read his reports, and the reports say there was a third car involved and that it looked as if you had been in the car with that woman who died, not in the same car as your sister."

Seth rubbed his temples. "She was my sister but never went to my room until a week after we'd been here?" What a convoluted mess. "And she claimed I was in her car, when the police think I was in Marjorie Lawson's car?"

The nurse nodded then sighed impatiently and began again. "When you get your records, unless someone has altered them, you should see the name of the doctor from California. Your sister called him and told Dr. Murrieta to work with him." Her eyes fluttered open. “Your sister was bossy and treated us like peasants, and I do not forget people like that. You were a good patient and very polite. That woman…forgive me, she was a bitch.” She looked apologetic, but only for a moment.

Seth bit back a smile. “Thank you. I appreciate your honesty.” He held out his hand for hers then kissed her fingertips, making her face flame with embarrassment, but he could tell he’d done the right thing. She had met enough rude Americans of late. It was time one of them treated her like a lady and gave her praise for her candor.

“One more thing,” she said. “As a favor to me, for helping you, señor? Please, don’t file charges against Dr. Martínez if he should not have operated on you. He donates his time to helping children who can’t afford medical services, and he sometimes takes pregnant women who have no place else to go. If he and that doctor from California did anything they shouldn’t have done, I don’t know that other man, but I’m sure Dr. Martínez only meant to help you.”

Seth watched her lips moving, and it was as if no sound came out of her mouth. The only thing he heard at first was a muffled sound…then nothing. She touched his arm, and Seth barely registered the sensation. “What?”

The nurse pulled him closer. “Are you okay? Did you hear anything I’ve just said the past few minutes?”

"Sure." Seth blinked. *It's happening again. Why can't I control the blank moments?*

Gómez indicated the elevator at the end of their walk. "Basement, turn right, the sign says Pesquisidor." She spelled it letter by letter to make certain he had it. "Have you had headaches lately?"

Seth shook his head. "Not really. Why?"

The nurse touched his forehead with the back of her hand. "It's the short-term memory, isn't it? I've seen this before—the patient talking with someone or walking somewhere, and all of a sudden they don't know what's going on or where they are for a moment." She smiled sadly. "You need to see a doctor. Maybe more imaging would help address the problem."

Seth thanked her again, then left, pulling Marjorie Lawson's photo from his pocket, ready to confront yet another official, hoping this one was more cooperative than the last and wondering how Charlie fared with the doctor.

Once he discovered how to reach the coroner's lab, Seth made his way to medical records to meet Charlie.

"WHAT DO YOU THINK?" Charlie asked when she met up with Seth outside the doors of the autopsy lab.

"I think we'll find an inaccurate summary of events fashioned in police vernacular," he replied grimly. He repeated what the nurse had told him. "It's in somebody's best interest not to be entirely truthful. Wonder why?"

Charlie held an innate need to defend police procedure, even if that of a foreign country, but she knew his skepticism was well founded. "I'd say somebody didn't want it to get out that they'd performed plastic surgery on the wrong man and that your accident may have been no accident."

She pulled out the pages they'd had copied of Seth's medical records. "If not for the badge and a phone call from Houston to Guadalajara, you realize we'd still be standing up there arguing, right?" She held out the forms for Seth to read.

He scanned them quickly, his body tensing. "It's as the nurse told me. Murrieta wasn't the one who requested I get my face overhauled—Dorinda did. But why? Knowing I'm not her brother, why would she go to the expense, for one thing?"

"You have no idea just how expensive," Charlie told him. "I pumped Murrieta for information about both of your surgeons, then phoned the office while I was waiting for you, and Julio got back to me with a brief profile on your chief surgeon, the California guy. He's one of those doctors to the stars, everything from breast implants to nose jobs, and he doesn't come cheaply."

"We're missing something," Seth murmured. "How do we prove I'm not Aldridge if I was the one on the operating table?"

Charlie had a thought. "You mentioned having a fit of sorts in your closet. How new are the clothes?"

"All of them brand new, some still with tags.

Why?" Then he brightened. "Pink, my butler, told me that before I came home, Dorinda and Doug went through that closet and tossed everything in it and ordered new clothing. Pink said he just thought it strange."

"When did he tell you this?" Charlie asked in surprise.

"Not long after we'd arrived in Houston. He was setting out clothes for me to wear one day, and I commented on how nothing looked familiar. He said one reason was because everything had been replaced."

"As if they'd bought clothes for a guy who couldn't wear the ones that were in the closet, someone who didn't live in that house," Charlie said.

"Exactly!" He scoffed. "That still makes no sense. Why not simply hire someone to impersonate him?"

"It makes sense if they've killed Aldridge," she told him. "Think about it. An accident, a man in a nearby room with no memory who has just come out of a coma, and he has no identification, no face, no memory. The perfect solution would be to convince him he's someone he's not rather than hire a third party, one who might talk later and maybe blackmail them."

"Pardon my ego for being offended that anyone could brainwash me. Besides. That's pretty thin," said Seth.

"Yeah, but 'thin' is my middle name. Not surprising according to my new partner who thinks I have terrible eating habits."

Seth frowned. "Which reminds me, we haven't eaten since we left Houston."

"Don't worry. I'll make you pay for starving me." She winked. "Right now, we need to get Marjorie Lawson's autopsy report—my captain has already spoken with the chief of police in Jalisco, so we should get out of here within minutes."

She was right. The state's medical examiner wasn't in, but his staff was quick to hand them the documents they wished for, almost as if getting them out of the hospital was more imperative than arguing with them. The documents were already copied and ready to hand over upon Charlie's signature. It was too clean, too quick and aroused Charlie's suspicions.

"You don't think someone tampered with the records, do you?" Seth asked after they'd left the office.

"I would hate to think so, but stranger things have happened." She stuffed the papers they'd just received into the folder with the others they'd collected in medical records. "The only things left to do are visit the hotel where Lawson stayed the night before she was killed and visit with your plastic surgeon, or the assistant, as the nurse called him. You up for it?"

"I'd rather grab a bite to eat," Seth said. "I already feel bad enough for keeping you out this late without lunch. I say we save the doctor for tomorrow and stop by the hotel on the way home tonight."

"Good. My stomach thinks my throat has been cut." Charlie winced, thinking of the George Martin case in Houston. "Sorry, bad choice of words."

Seth seemed to have noticed her demeanor. "I speak fluent hunger, no problem. Why the grimace, though? Thinking of a case?"

"One that has had me baffled for some time," she admitted. "And I'm tempted to have Julio, my partner, send me some things on it so I can look him up here. The man was on his way to Mexico when he died, according to the one witness I have who knew him. I'd like to know what his business was here. I just think it's strange that he dies en route, you almost die once you get here, and none of the information I've gotten supports a damned thing as far as motive for any of it. Does the name George Martin name ring a bell?"

"Nope. But both are common names, no?" Seth rolled his head from side to side, popping his neck. He groaned. "Hell, I don't know. Not like I've read books on the subject."

"If that's even his name." She rubbed her temples. "I'm starting to think that your family and his should go bowling, maybe come up with some believable scenarios as to why it is there is so little information on either of you and how Mexico figures into it."

"One more thing." He paused. "Where were you

going with the conversation when you asked about the clothes in my closet?"

"Ah, yes." Charlie tapped her forehead. "If you had any of Aldridge's old clothes, his toothbrush, a comb, something with his DNA, we could compare it to yours. If that's out of the question, we could always do a comparison of yours to Dorinda's."

Seth gave her a quick hug. "For that little gem of detective know-how, I'll even spring for dessert. C'mon."

"Do you have any of those things we can test?" she asked worriedly.

Seth thought a moment. "There's a pair of shoes they missed in the back of one of the closets. I wasn't sure whose they were and why they were there. Sort of forgot about it until now. There are watches and ties that would have fit either of us. Maybe those aren't new?"

"Worth a shot." Charlie chewed her bottom lip, thinking. "There has to be something else."

Seth snapped his fingers. "Of course—tams, fedoras, golf caps. I don't wear hats, at least I don't think I do. But there are several on the top shelves of the closets—I put them up there when I saw them, because...like I said...not my thing. Surely Aldridge wore at least one of them. There has to be DNA in there that we could use."

She thought a moment. "You said golf hats—that means..." Her eyes widened.

"Golf clubs!" they cried in unison.

"Yep, more fingerprints." Then Charlie halted him. "We have to go back to the hospital and pull Dorinda's medical files to get her information. It won't be easy, considering what we went through to get yours."

"Call your captain and have him get started on it," Seth suggested. "We'll eat, come back here, look up the assistant plastic surgeon, then check Marjorie Lawson's hotel on the way back to our own."

"You owe me a B&B when this is all over," Charlie told him on the way back to their car. "A major bourbon and backrub."

She stopped walking and faced him. "By the way, why is it you never drive? Not even before the accident?"

He frowned. "I have no clue. Maybe I'm a gigolo who enjoys being pampered."

Charlie snorted. "As reticent as you are to initiate intimacy?"

He looked surprised and then hurt. "I wasn't aware you wanted..."

"Skip it. Sorry." Flustered, she did her best to change the subject. *When did this happen? You're on a job—this isn't a personal mission.*

CHAPTER SIX

ONCE THEY'D EATEN, securing Dorinda Wilkerson's information was more difficult than they'd imagined. The hospital contacted the police, and their chief had to be placated by Houston PD and reassured that nothing the Mexican department had done was suspect, that the Texans were simply working a case involving possible deception on the part of an American citizen living there.

Charlie's crime lab already had Seth's DNA on file, so the results would be ready before the two of them landed in Texas after their weekend in Mexico.

"I must admit something," she said on their way to the distressed area of Guadalajara where Rodrigo Martínez devoted his time helping inner city children. "People complain about their jobs all the time—I like mine, but I'm even more thankful that I work in Houston instead of here."

She surveyed the crowded, graffiti-decorated streets as they passed through, conscious of the wary looks everyone between the ages of six and seventy gave them, staring, not only as if they distrusted them but as if they were contemplating pulling a weapon and taking their car. Even the kids looked capable enough to pull off such an act.

"I don't think they see too many gringos in this neighborhood," Seth said quietly. "You sure you want to get out? I could go in by myself."

"Not a chance." She tapped the gun at her side lightly. "I'm your detail, remember? You aren't carrying a gun."

"Maybe I know how to protect myself without bullets," he said.

"And maybe you're just full of it. I'm going inside with you. Our driver can lock his doors and call the zero-whatever number for emergency if he's scared." She snorted indelicately. "Might not be a bad idea to hand him the number to the American consulate in case we don't come back in a timely manner."

Their driver, whose name she hadn't gotten, evidently spoke English. He'd been silent during their entire trip with him, but now he looked into the rearview mirror, his straightforward gaze catching her attention, and he spoke in perfect English. "We have concealed carry laws in Mexico." Then he pulled out a massive pistol from beneath his seat, quickly and smoothly enough that Charlie instinctively grabbed her own gun. The look he shot her was humorous as he returned the gun to where he'd had it. "I have permits."

Charlie and Seth exchanged surprised looks. The small, unobtrusive man who'd been driving them carried a firearm that looked as if it could put a basketball-sized hole in a tank.

"Where did you find him?" she asked quietly from the corner of her mouth, settling her Glock back into its holster.

Seth never took his eyes from their chauffer but shrugged. "Phonebook?"

"I thought it was impossible to get one of those," Charlie ventured, speaking to their driver.

He grinned. "Not if you have the right lawyer. The size of the pistola is what can be questionable, but I belong to a sportsman's club, so I have permission to carry this one and my *escopetas*… You say shotguns."

"Ah." She returned his smile, unnerved but unwilling to let him know. Yeah, the guy would be able to take care of himself and their car.

He stopped the sedan before a sickly-looking pink building that said Dispensario and announced that they were at the free clinic. Barefoot children ran, laughing, back and forth in front of the building, cocking their fingers like guns and pulling imaginary triggers. Shoving and pushing one another playfully until they spotted the adults sitting in the car.

Charlie popped Seth lightly on the leg, encouraging him to exit so she could get out. The sooner they completed their business in this part of the city the better, especially since it would soon be dark. The atmosphere was ominous enough with the impending thunderstorms. She'd heard the sky rumbling off and on for several minutes, and the swirling clouds overhead indicated a major storm, unless she missed her guess.

On their way from the car to the medical facility, fat raindrops fell on them and splattered near their feet. Charlie shook her hair once inside the door and shivered. Between the weather and that driver holding a gun that could fell a buffalo, she had gooseflesh. She rubbed her arms to take away some of the chill.

Seth chuckled. "Never underestimate the quiet ones. He's probably got shoulder-fired rocket launchers, grenades and Belgian assault rifles in his car trunk."

Charlie lifted an eyebrow. "You are definitely a Fed. I have yet to see you fingering fabrics or playing with a color chart, so the idea that you may be an interior decorator is moot."

He opened the door for her. "Thank God. If it takes me several months to figure out I don't have denim in the house, imagine how lousy I'd be at coordinating anything else."

The inside of the building was even worse than the outside, with pockets of flooring ripped up and dirt where cement or boards should be. Charlie would be surprised if there was running water or electricity. The only thing she took comfort in was that there didn't appear to be pestilence. Whoever cared for the building seemed to have made certain that as many precautions as possible had been taken to ensure the best health care for those who showed up, despite the impoverished conditions.

They walked in the general direction of voices that could be heard echoing down the empty corridors. The building seemed to be an abandoned school because there were small chairs and tables here and there, stacked in corners of empty rooms. Dusty bookcases stood sentry just within rooms where doors had once hung on hinges but where now only bolts jutted from broken, jagged frames.

She sniffed indelicately, her nostrils smelling and tongue tasting a weird mixture of antiseptic and old, cold dirt.

Seth touched her arm and pointed at an open door. Beyond the entrance, in a room lit only by natural light through dirty windows, was a man in a white lab coat and three people who looked to be a mother and two children, both boys.

Out of respect for the mother, Charlie held up a hand, silently requesting Seth to wait before entering. They waited, watching, as the doctor finished his examination and in hushed tones gave the woman verbal instructions and pressed something into her hands. Probably medicine for the boy.

The Mexican woman shepherded her children single file past the two Americans and averted her eyes while the doctor stared warily from inside the sparse room.

Charlie held out her hand and introduced herself. Seth did the same.

Dr. Martínez seemed frightened at first, then angry. He held up his hands. "I received a phone call from the state's coroner yesterday, telling me you would be here."

"And?" Charlie looked from him to Seth then back to the doctor. Were they already conspiring to hide evidence?

"There's no need for your concern as to why you received the surgeries—you would have been disfigured, unable to go anywhere without causing a stir. Perhaps some of it was unnecessary, such as breaking your jaw when it was fine, but the skin grafts and such… We had to do this. As for who suggested your operations and who paid for them, I don't believe there should be secrecy," the doctor explained. "I am a good man. An honest man." He looked at Seth. "I helped give you a better quality of life than you'd have had without the surgeries on your face."

Charlie assured him that she and Seth never had any doubts of that. "We're just here to find out who signed the paperwork for his surgeries, how you were brought into this, and why he was told his name was Mason Aldridge when it's not."

"The American woman insisted, and who were we to disagree?" Martínez asked. "She offered money, lots of it, if we would just perform the surgeries and not ask any questions." He looked at Seth and took a deep breath. "I am sorry if this has hurt you, but you received the best medical treatment possible. We worked many hours—there were so many broken bones and the torn skin. We felt grateful to have been able to make you look as you do."

He seemed to be examining his work as he spoke to Seth, lifting a hand to touch Seth's face and turn it this way and that, slowly, like he was studying a fine sculpture. "You healed nicely."

"Thanks." Seth sounded as if he meant it, but Charlie wondered if she detected a note of hostility. Not that she'd blame him.

"You say this American woman offered you money?" Charlie asked.

"What she paid your chief surgeon, I have no idea—it is none of my business. As for me? Two hundred fifty thousand for a new clinic. We've started building but were shut down because of the rains last month," explained Martínez. "The new structure is two blocks to the north." He added, as if qualifying once again his part in the deception, "A quarter of a million dollars is a lot of money in Mexico, especially for this community."

"We don't want to cause you any problems, Dr. Martínez," Charlie told him. "We're just looking for the truth so we can clear up some things back in Houston."

Seth surveyed the room and nodded. "You and the people you help deserve a better environment. You won't have any trouble from us. We won't be involving the police, here or in the States."

Martínez breathed what was obviously a sigh of relief. He nodded, and his eyes welled with tears. He choked when trying to speak. "Thank you."

"You're welcome." Seth nodded as he spoke. "I do have a favor to ask. I need copies of my medical records, anything you've signed describing the procedures, who signed the permission slips, that sort of thing."

"Of course. I'll phone my office. It's open tomorrow until noon if you can be there to pick them up by then. We don't have a lot of money for postage to send them to the States for you."

Seth shook the physician's hand once more, then ushered Charlie out the door and down the hall. "I wonder how our driver is doing," he commented.

The meeting with Martínez had been more emotional for Charlie than anything she'd encountered in a long while. She was glad Seth had put him at ease, that he hadn't been upset. Many men and women would have raised hell had someone altered their appearance to the extent Martínez and his California accomplice had done. She could barely drag her thoughts from the medical snafu with Seth to the man waiting for them outside the door.

"As long he's there and hasn't left us," she said. "I don't know enough Spanish, even having spoken it on the job, to bail us out if we get into trouble here."

They rounded the corner from the hall they'd taken and opened the door leading outside. To Charlie's relief, their driver was not only there, he was tossing a ball with some of the children who'd been running in the street when they'd pulled up to the clinic. The rain seemed to have stopped momentarily. The streets were still slick, but the sun was peeking through the clouds.

Their driver said something to the children in Spanish, opened the sedan's doors and within minutes had them moving out of the inner city and back to the highway they'd taken on their way there.

Charlie felt weak. She'd eaten hurriedly hours earlier, but the day's events seemed to be taking their toll. She hadn't had but a short while to assimilate the information they'd collected nor to manage her scattered thoughts on having Seth back. Several cases had drained her physically, but none had slammed her as emotionally as this one. She'd still not asked the police in Mexico about George Martin, whether or not they knew of him.

Nothing that can't be handled once you're back in Houston, Charlie. She settled against the leather seat and tried stilling the thoughts that made her brain ache. Was there a connection between Seth and Martin? If so...what? Had they worked together? Were they both part of the same law enforcement agency, or had one been after the other in a sting operation of some sort? She'd have to ask Gloria, the witness, the woman who had come to her last year, saying she'd been a friend of Martin's and believed she knew who had killed him.

Whenever Charlie had asked who, the woman

had replied that all Martin had told her was that his boss was involved. But the man, Damien Rogers, had claimed Martin had only worked for him, that he knew nothing about his disappearance, much less his death. That had been over a year ago.

Seth reached for her hand and pulled it into his, lacing fingers with her. "What are you thinking?"

"I'm wondering about the cold case I mentioned to you earlier. I haven't spoken with the Mexican police about Martin, and I need to do that before we leave."

"Can it wait until tomorrow?"

"It'll have to." She was immediately sorry she sounded so short. "It's more important that we do what we're doing today. I can always phone them from Houston or ask my captain to intervene."

When he didn't respond, she glanced upward. He was staring at what looked like empty space, and he had a faraway look in his eyes, as if he wasn't there but millions of miles away.

"Seth?" She had to call his name twice before he looked at her.

"Hmm?" he finally responded.

She squeezed his hand. "We can't handle the hotels and doctors as easily from home as we can while we're here. I'm just cranky. This case has me baffled."

He stroked the inside of her wrist slowly. "Sure that's not all that's upsetting you?"

An obnoxious thunderclap reverberated like a slap

from God, its noise keeping her from answering. The car trembled, and their driver fought to maintain control. Rain seemed to fall in buckets, flooding the streets, slamming the windshield with a force that obliterated their vision. Charlie pitched against Seth, whose arms shot around her protectively.

The sky darkened so quickly that if she had blinked, it wouldn't have been as fast as the change in the weather. For the first time since stepping onto Mexican soil, Charlie was frightened. Not of the people, the neighborhood from which they'd just come or not understanding the language and customs, but of the forces of nature that seemed angry enough to destroy them all.

She glanced at Seth. The last time he'd been in Mexico there had been a storm. He had to be thinking of that night, because whether or not he recalled the events, he remembered the irrevocable aftermath that changed his life. Maybe that's why he'd seemed to space out moments earlier.

"Hey!" Seth called to their driver.

The man didn't speak but acknowledged Seth by meeting his eyes in his mirror briefly.

"What's your name?" Seth asked.

"Guillermo. William."

"William, how would you feel about spending the night in a motel next door to us?" Seth waved his free hand at the storm outside their car. "I'll pay for your room, your dinner, and I'll throw in an extra couple hundred dollars for your trouble. Five if you'll go for supper and bring us back a nice meal."

William nodded. "Want me to find a place?"

"Please." Seth's body visibly relaxed. Charlie could feel the tension ease in the hand that held hers and in the thigh that brushed hers.

William chuckled. "We have what the locals call love motels. Pay by the hour or by the night. There are a couple close by."

"As long as they don't have bugs or spiders, and as long as they aren't easily compromised," Seth said. "Sure, why not?"

"They're very nice. Even provide toothbrushes and condoms."

William lowered his head after speaking and feigned concentrating on the road, but Charlie saw him cut his eyes upward now and then, gauging her reaction.

Most likely because I gasped, thought Charlie. She couldn't suppress a smile, though, because she was sure that in his mind, William had been chatting with another male passenger and had forgotten about the female in the backseat.

Oh, perfect, a storm. And a motel with toothbrushes and condoms. Whoopee. Just what I've wanted. With pretty lingerie she rarely got the chance to wear, a new pair of sandals to show off the ankle bracelet she hadn't worn in over two years and her favorite perfume back at the posh hotel where their luggage sat, unpacked and waiting.

Her eyes grew wide, and she stifled another gasp as William pulled into a motel's single exit/entrance. This was like some circus ride. Jump in, jump off after the ride was over. She was positive many a man had taken his mistress to this place.

Seth handed over a credit card when William let the electric window down, and the attendant took their information, then swiped the card and directed them to two of the units, side by side. Charlie giggled despite herself. She was sure the attendant received many visitors with a variety of kinky preferences, but she'd never imagined herself going to a love motel with two men, one of whom didn't remember her and the other a stranger.

William pulled into an open cavern-looking place then pressed a hand-held electronic device that the attendant had given him, and a massive garage door closed behind them. Once he'd killed the engine, William stepped out and opened the door.

Charlie was amazed. The garage floor was tiled, and the ceiling was bóveda, made of bricks that had been widely arched.

Past the garage was a spacious, inviting apartment with a bed, kitchenette and large bathroom. As William had said, there was a basket full of everything a couple would want…for a few hours or a night. Charlie picked up the guest soap and sniffed, surprised and pleased. Maybe this wouldn't be so bad after all.

SETH COULD HAVE DONE without William's sly comment about the condoms being available, but he hadn't wanted to brave the storm looking for a different place to crash. He figured he should feel guilty for sending William back into the storm for food, but a local eatery could provide plenty for the three of them, and the trip would be safer and quicker for the driver, who had left only moments earlier, saying he'd be back within the hour with supplies.

Seth sat on the edge of the first bed he came to and leaned against the inviting softness. The mattress was well-worn but not uncomfortable. Yeah, he could fall asleep here.

He sat up, however, not willing to be the first to fall asleep, not when he was responsible for Charlie's safety and comfort. Some trip he'd provided. He'd had her travel hundreds of miles without feeding her until she looked as if she could pass out. He'd had her traipse all over both a clean, modern hospital and a grungy, inner city clinic where they could have been mugged or killed. She'd been a trooper, flashing her smile and her badge, helping him get the information he needed. Sure, she said she was also working on a cold case from Houston, but he knew she was primarily there to support him and help him find answers to the questions his mind could barely conceive.

"Did you bring in the folder…the information we secured today?" he asked.

Charlie patted the stack of papers she'd set on the

table next to a small television. She hadn't moved once they'd entered the room.

He looked at her apologetically. "I'd have ordered nice weather if it'd been an option," he said.

"I know that." She smiled. "It is what it is, as a friend of mine says." She kicked off her shoes and came to sit beside him on the bed. "Besides, it's all in a day's work."

"I didn't bring you here for that," he said, lifting a strand of damp hair from her brow.

"Yeah? Why did you bring me to Mexico?" Her voice was calm, but he saw the pulse jump in her throat, and he longed to taste the smooth skin.

"Maybe this wasn't such a good idea," he said, rising.

Charlie sought his hand and pulled him back onto the bed beside her. "That was a provocative question—sorry. I didn't mean to flirt."

He looked at her small hand on his larger one then into her eyes. "Don't misunderstand me. I want you. I'm just afraid of rushing things with you. I know I must've done something that hurt you, but I haven't a clue what it was."

"You disappeared." She shrugged. "Not like you could help it if you were knocked unconscious...and hurt." Her brows puckered into a frown.

"You wonder—so do I, if it makes you feel any better," he said. "You want to know what I was doing here and if I was with another woman, with Marjorie Lawson."

"She was pretty. I've seen you studying her photograph."

He nodded. "I'd like to know what she meant to me, whether we were friends, coworkers, whatever. I just can't remember."

"We'll find out. We still have time to go to her hotel tomorrow."

Seth was pretty sure he didn't smoke, but at the moment he'd have given anything for a cigarette, something to do with his hands and occupy the thoughts that had derailed somewhere during their flight into Mexico. "Do you have any idea what it's like to fear your own mind, to know there are secrets hidden somewhere between yesterday and tomorrow if only you could find the key?"

Charlie shook her head slowly.

"Well, I do. Haven't a clue why my disappearance in Mexico has anything to do with you, but I know it does, and the whole tangled web needs unraveling before I can find any peace."

She tapped his forearm then splayed her hands before him. "Go over what we know for sure. I'll handle our relationship—you tackle your memory problems."

"I don't get it." He frowned.

"You will. Pretend we're in elementary school and have to use our fingers to represent numbers or thoughts. What's the first thing you remember?"

Seth held up his forefinger. "That's easy. I woke up in a Mexican hospital and didn't recognize the people who claimed we were related." He held up a second finger. "I had no memory of the face that stared back at me when I looked in the mirror." A third finger rose. "All I had on me that seemed familiar was a telephone number. Yours."

Charlie ticked off items on her own hand, one finger at a time. "All I know is that one day you were with me, saying you had to go to Mexico on business. Months later, after having not heard from you, suddenly I get a phone call and it's you, even though you don't remember me or anything about our relationship." She thought a moment before continuing, "As for what happened in the meantime..." She frowned. "No. This happened before you left. I was working a cold case on Martin." She looked up. "Come to think of it, that's about the time you entered the picture. Seems I hadn't been working the Martin file long before you and I met."

It occurred to Seth that he might not want to know the answer to the question forming in his mind, but he had to ask, "Did you ever tell me that George Martin disappeared in Mexico?"

She looked around their room before speaking again. "Our flight doesn't leave until evening. Why did you only pay for this suite?"

Did she just brush aside the possibility I might be connected to something she'd been working on? Seth considered her question, but he had no ready answer. It hadn't occurred to him she might want a room of her own. Of course she would. He shook his head. “I could always crash with William.”

“Uh-uh. I only wondered if it was an automatic reaction or if you’d thought about it.”

“Honestly? It never crossed my mind. It was storming, and we’re in a foreign country. I guess I wanted to protect you. Strange, huh? You’re the one with the gun and the badge, but I guess I have to be a macho—”

Charlie shocked the hell out of him by what she did next. She covered his mouth, first with her hand, then as she climbed onto his lap, she replaced her fingers with her lips. The kiss was his undoing. Long-suppressed need, barely beneath the surface of his consciousness, rose as he possessed her.

His tongue slipped between her teeth and caressed the interior of her mouth, burning her, claiming her, spearing every inch he could find. The soft, warm heat of her lips against his drove him insane with a yearning he’d felt since meeting her at the restaurant. Seth’s arms slipped over and around her, and he lay back on the bed, dragging her on top of him then rolling to his side where he could cradle her while making love to her.

She was his salvation, the one true comfort he’d felt in months, her presence a blanket that surrounded and held him a willing captive. Her tiny hands touched his chest, burning through his shirt, searing his heart. So small yet so powerful. Hands that he knew could probably rip him into shreds or mold him to suit her needs.

"Do you remember this?" she said on a sigh, pulling his shirt from his pants and slipping her hands around to caress his back, sliding them slowly upward over his aching muscles. She lifted her face to kiss him again, softly, tenderly, but passionately. Then she pulled back, raking his back slightly with her nails, grinding her hips against him. "Or this?"

"Yes," he whispered, kissing her again before she could pull away from him to tease him further. He held her firmly, his heat striving of its own accord, seeking entrance to the sweet folds he knew were mere inches away.

Charlie tossed her head, twisting and turning above him. She gasped as their lips parted, and she asked him, "Really? Is this something you know or wish?"

"Both." He couldn't stop kissing her. Her writhing body, her scent, everything about her called to him, and he couldn't resist, couldn't deny the attraction, didn't care if his body recalled what his mind couldn't or if his brain tricked him into believing the oasis was real.

Only a fool would break the spell, would admit he wasn't one hundred percent positive that he knew the woman in his arms and that he adored and missed her desperately.

Seth pulled back. *Yeah, and only a jerk would let*

her believe what she wants, what we both want but can't prove.

"William will be back in a bit," he said gruffly, fighting for self-control. "I don't want to put you in a compromising position when he gets here."

Charlie blinked. "Sure." She rose quickly and bolted for the bathroom, straightening her clothing. She was gone before he could call her back, to attempt explaining that she hadn't done anything wrong, that it was him and his own reluctance to involve her any deeper in his problems than he already had. When she was with him, he wanted her passion, not her pity; her love, not her consolation.

Seth lay on the bed, regulating his breathing and berating himself for being seven kinds of fool. He was screwed no matter what he did. He only hoped she knew it, too, and that she forgave him.

THE MAN IS AN IDIOT. Charlie splashed cold water on her face, more to soothe the sting of his rejection than to cool her flaming face. *You're no better,* she told herself. He was walking, talking, breathing, but he wasn't fully living. For whatever his reasons, his life was similar to hers, on hold. *And here you are, waiting for him to make the moves on you.*

She stayed in the bathroom, rehashing old memories and present circumstances, trying to think of a way to reach him, to reconnect with the man she'd known. When she heard him talking to William and heard the driver leave to go to his own room, only then did she reemerge, entering the bedroom suite as if nothing had happened.

The meal, however, was a somber affair. The monsoon-like winds and rain raged outside while their personal storm seethed within the walls of the apartment, building with every bite they ate and every breath they took. They barely spoke. She could hardly choke down her meal.

After they'd finished and she helped clear the small table where they'd dined, Charlie took the top sheet from the bed and went to the bathroom again, this time to shower and fashion a toga out of the only material available, considering they had no fresh clothes. She stood beneath the steaming water until she realized she was chilled. Her thoughts had occupied her so that she hadn't noticed when bathing stopped and passing time began. It wasn't like her to stand still, quiet, reserved, without emotion.

She surveyed the small basket in the bathroom that held toiletries. Choosing one of the toothbrushes, she performed her usual evening ritual, still taking her time. *If he's waiting, let him stew.*

As soon as she emerged and went toward the bed, the look in his eyes both charmed and alarmed her. She felt simultaneously like the hunter and the hunted.

That's what bugged her the most. She felt like a big game hunter stalking a large, sleek cat, and she couldn't make up her mind whether she wanted to trap him and train him, or have him catch her and just have his way with her. Either way equaled unparalleled fun, both avenues promised to be maddening and the outcome would be the same. They'd wind up with a stormy love affair that would keep their adrenaline pumping until they were octogenarians.

Provided the alpha cat got off his butt and made a move on her, because it wasn't her in her nature to be the blasted hunter.

Charlie wrapped the sheet more securely about her and climbed into bed, doing her best to ignore him as he unbuttoned his still-damp shirt and draped it over the back of a chair. She reached for the television remote, feeling him staring at her, and she knew he wanted to talk but didn't know where to begin.

And I'm damned if I'll help him. She ran her fingers through her hair, testing its dryness, still conscious of him watching, so she tilted her head slightly, parted her lips, preening, exposing her neck and executing a vulnerable pose, much like a wanton lady tempting a vampire.

She slid him a look from the corner of her eyes. He looked like he wanted to bite her all right.

When he started pacing, slowly at first, then with more energy as the storm outside intensified in sound and fury, he really did look like a big cat, and the sight of his half-naked torso did more than arouse an animalistic sensation in her body.

Charlie stifled a groan and focused harder on

whatever was on the tube. *Why can't I remember what I just watched?* She peered more intently.

A sound resembling that of a growl emanated from Seth's direction. Charlie glanced up and found him staring at her, his eyes unfathomable, dark and broody.

"What?" she finally asked.

"I don't want to hurt you." The words were quiet, firm, drained of any emotion she could identify.

Anger, pain and frustration bubbled up, and Charlie leapt from the bed to stand before him. "Too… late!" She balled up her fist and socked him on the shoulder.

"What?" He looked incredulous.

She hated herself for trembling, for standing before him naked except for a thin motel sheet. "You broke my heart." Her voice cracked on the last syllable, and she shuddered uncontrollably.

The look on Seth's face was painful to behold. She could tell that he, as well, felt wounded, and it was obvious he didn't know what to do about it.

Charlie grabbed him by the belt and backed him toward the bed. Lifting the hem of her toga, she swooped a leg behind his, buckling his knees and landing him on the bed. Instead of climbing on top of him this time, however, she leaned over, fuming.

"Still think I can't take care of myself?" she asked. "Think you're going to hurt me?"

She reached into her purse on the nightstand and grabbed her handcuffs, and before she could think rationally, she snapped one link around one of his wrists and in one motion flipped him onto his stomach and grabbed his other wrist, securing it with the other steel band.

Seth bellowed in protest, and she jerked him back to face her.

"Oh, shut up," she admonished. "I promise not to hurt you and not to make you wear these all night. I just wanted to prove something, you big dope. I may be small, but I can handle you and whatever problems you toss at me. I'm not afraid of street thugs, murderers and rapists, so what makes you think I can't handle an amnesiac with a guilt complex?"

The outright indignation on Seth's face was enough to make her back away, but his mercurial physical response was the biggest surprise. Before Charlie could budge, he'd twisted his torso, performed what had to be a painful dislocation of his shoulders. He rolled her onto her back with the strength of his thighs, pinning her, his eyes blazing into hers, defying her, stripping her bare, and she had no doubt that had he wanted, he could have killed her.

Tremors of shock raced down her spine, and his crushing weight stole her breath, weakening her defenses, both physically and emotionally. She knew, even with his weight crushing her, that she could wriggle out of the entrapment, but not without hurting him further, so she lay still.

"I appreciate your concern for my sensitive guilt

complex," he said evenly, "but if you don't mind, I'll deal with it in my own time, my way, without your interference or input. If I want to know what you think about how I'm handling my neuroses, I'll ask you." He bent his head and crushed her lips in a punishing kiss. She didn't miss his wince or groan.

After making sure she was submissive enough not to lash back at him, he lifted his head. "Now. Where's the damned key to these cuffs before I pass out and we're both hurting?"

Charlie swallowed hard, barely able to breathe. She shifted her gaze to somewhere behind him, her voice scarcely audible. "In my purse."

"Get them." It wasn't a request.

He rolled, taking her with him to an upright position.

She staggered trying to stand, so she plopped back onto the side of the bed, digging into her purse with shaking fingers until she snagged her keys. Unlocking the handcuffs, she avoided his gaze, feeling the heat from his stare blazing against her face.

He glared at her. "Next time you want to handcuff me, lady, you'd better be prepared to spend the night that way. Got it?"

Charlie nodded, flushing. Somebody didn't like being confined. Not that she blamed him. It was a stupid thing for her to do. Illegal, had they been in the States, maybe even in Mexico. She should be ashamed, but instead…she was intrigued, and to her chagrin…a little turned on. Wow.

What was it he'd said when they first encountered William with his pistol?

Never underestimate the quiet ones.

While she corralled her own thoughts, she watched as he confirmed her suspicions. He had dislocated his shoulders in order to trap her. Seth walked to the bathroom door and slammed himself against the doorjamb. A muffled but gut-wrenching sound emanated from him, and she heard the sound of bone against bone as well as flesh against wood as he realigned the bones he'd discombobulated.

The thought that he'd been able to do such a thing was spooky. That he'd done it so quickly was unnerving, making her wonder about the job he'd had when they met. Was he some sort of Harry Houdini thief, possibly a cat burglar used to getting in and out of tight places, or a highly-trained spook for the government?

Had Seth been involved in some accident as a youth or young man, one in which he'd had his arms nearly ripped from their sockets? Was he double-jointed? Nobody she knew had the ability to do such a thing.

Other than the initial grunted moan he'd given when he first fired his body like a human missile at the door frame, he hadn't made a sound. Charlie couldn't tear her gaze from his. No reaction other than the same expressionless stare he'd exhibited on the bed—dark, dangerous and most definitely defiant.

She knew she'd screwed up so she offered what she could to diffuse the situation. "I have some pain-killers in my purse. Want them?"

CHAPTER SEVEN

THE REMAINDER OF THE NIGHT was pure hell on Seth. First he'd come close to taking Charlie, against his better judgment, knowing he couldn't commit to memories that were still sketchy and knowing she needed to know he remembered every move, every utterance. He wanted to remember—he craved knowing, but all he had were fragmented pieces floating somewhere just beyond his reach.

Then, when he'd been about to explode from need of her, the little witch had handcuffed him, chastised him and accused him of nursing his ego, of all things.

His groin still ached from unrequited want. Almost as bad as his friggin' shoulders. He hoped uncharitably that she wasn't entirely comfortable in the bed while he had crashed on the floor near her feet.

He asked himself over and over, did he want her because he remembered her, remembered them, or was he so hot he nearly combusted every time she looked at him because he hadn't been with a woman since God knew when?

Seth shook his head restlessly. No, it was obviously because of Charlie somehow. No other woman had affected him quite the way she did—of that much he was positive. He admired her professionalism when interviewing the doctors, her panache at adapting to the horrid weather conditions and her spunk at taking him down a notch or two when he got under her skin.

What he felt when he held her, kissed her or merely looked at her was an entirely different matter, one dealing with parts of himself he hadn't known existed. She got to him with her direct gazes and mocking grin, the way she placed her hands on her hips when she was thinking, how she had no problem eating in front of him, which was refreshing. The few women he'd encountered since he left Mexico were so self-conscious they couldn't enjoy themselves. Not so with Charlie. She was in the moment no matter when or where she was.

Someone's cell phone rang. He smacked his forehead at the chance that it might be his—who would be calling him? Dorinda? Fat chance. She'd probably discovered he was gone within an hour of his having left the mansion the night before, but he was confident neither Hector nor Pink would give him up, and Dorinda didn't have this particular cell phone number.

The darkened room brightened slightly when he heard the bedside lamp click on. He listened to Charlie's soft, low voice and determined she was in deep discussion with her partner. What had she called him?

"Julio, slow down. Where did you get this information?" she asked quietly.

Seth leaned so far from his pallet beneath her that he feared she'd see his head poking around the corner, spying on her. He glanced at the alarm clock on her bedside table. Five minutes of midnight. He hoped she chewed Julio's ass for waking them. Then again, it irked him that the man felt free enough to phone her in the middle of the damned night, even if he was her partner.

When it appeared she was saying goodbye, he quickly dove back beneath the thin blanket and eased his head back onto the single pillow she'd tossed him from the bed. Her silence bugged him. What was she thinking? What had Julio said that was so upsetting?

Seth waited a few seconds before breaking the silence. "Everything okay?"

"Not really. That was my partner—he's working late, said a body was found slashed and stuffed in a Dumpster near one of the yacht clubs. Seems my one witness in the George Martin case was murdered."

"Witness? How strong?" he asked.

"She's the one who told me Martin was on his way to Mexico last time they spoke. He was at Bush Airport, about to board the plane when he called to let her know he'd be gone a few days on business, something to do with the escort service."

He heard Charlie sigh and remained silent. He knew Charlie was wondering whether the Martin case impacted his own...if what he had could be considered a case. He wasn't a part of anyone's investigation, no police report had been filed, and if he had enemies, he wouldn't remember them anyway.

"Charlie?" he asked softly.

"I'm okay."

Seth had no choice but to take Charlie at her word. Not that she'd have let him comfort her if she was upset, but it was worth being the one to break their silence to let her know he was there.

Seconds later, the dimly lit room went dark as Charlie turned off the light one last time. For one idiotic moment, Seth thought he heard her sob.

Nah. She's not the type. No woman who faces down...how did she put it? Street thugs, murderers and rapists. That woman wouldn't let something like a witness's demise get to her like that.

SHE'D HAD MORE restful nights sleeping on her father's lumpy couch, less doubts about herself at thirteen, when all her friends were getting their periods and she was the Lone Ranger with a flat chest and no visits from Mother Nature.

Nothing like driving through a blistering storm, having the man who proposed to you turn you down in bed and your partner calling with news that your cold case just went into deep freeze—all within a matter of hours. How did the old saying go? A day that had been a total waste of makeup.

Her one consolation was that she and Seth would soon be flying home, that she could get back to work on the Martin case and either investigate Wanda Schoonover's murder or regrettably close the darned thing out, chalking up months of hard work to just that, tons of work on a job that just didn't bring the desired results. Not all of them turned out well—she knew that when she joined the department.

And what of Seth Taggart? Was she willing to give up on the one relationship in her life that had held promise, hope, desire and passion? The hell of it was that he hadn't abandoned her…them. Nothing like that. It was simply as if they'd never existed, never loved.

The relationship hadn't died, so there was no body to mourn, no goodbyes left unsaid, just the memories that—in the only analogy she could conjure—were becoming more and more like some pastry with the filling torn out of it. She knew what she'd tasted had been sweet, and she'd looked forward to devouring all of it, but after one bite, she found herself betrayed. Not by the food itself, but by some invisible yet painfully tangible knowledge that she was left empty and wanting. And there didn't seem to be a damned thing she could do about it.

The storm had died, and the two of them still had much to do before boarding their return flight, but Charlie resented having to work in the same clothes she'd worn the day before when she had clean clothing, toiletries, makeup and perfume back at the other hotel.

Seth didn't look much better than she felt. He'd

hung his clothing in the bathroom and let steam from his morning shower help with some of the wrinkles and signs of usage, but she'd seen him looking more rested and fresh.

They had all but avoided one another since rising. Whereas they'd at least been civil the night before, even after she'd handcuffed him and he'd rebuffed her, the tension between them today was a thick fog of misunderstanding and unspoken feelings. She had half a mind to toss him back onto the bed and force him to deal with her before they drove across town to see what the staff of Hotel Álcazar had to say about Ms. Lawson's short stay there.

"I know it seems I'm always apologizing for not feeding you," Seth began, "but I just want to get out of here, check with the hotel and see what we can do about piecing some of this together if that's okay."

"Sure." She knew how he felt. Business first, then pack and get home.

Seth, however, surprised her. "I want to spend another day here."

Charlie scoffed. "I can't take off work."

"You don't have to be back until Monday. Tomorrow is Friday so that gives us plenty of time if we take the red-eye home Sunday night. I promise I'll treat you to some decent meals, even give you that bourbon and backrub you said I owed you. But we can get more accomplished here than we can back in Houston."

He hadn't said please, but she could see a hint of imploring behind those smoky-colored eyes.

"Seth, if this is about last night, there's no need for..."

He stopped what he was doing and walked toward her. At first, she thought he was about to kiss her, but he lifted his arms and caught a towel falling off the rack directly behind her that would have landed on her head.

Slowly, he replaced the item, his body pressing against hers, triggering her response to flee. When he looked down the length of his nose at her, she knew he saw the heat coming from her face. Why couldn't she keep from blushing every time he was near?

Seth's lips parted. "I know that. This isn't an apology or a goodwill gesture."

She felt her nostrils flare as she remained silent, refusing to let her wounded heart overcome her common sense. "Then what is it?"

He dipped his head, brushing his mouth against hers. "You tell me." She felt his hands resting gently on her shoulders then tensing when their lips touched.

Seth's tongue flicked out to taste her lips. "All I know is that I've done my best to keep from hurting you. Then you talk to Julio, or whoever he is, on the phone, and the two of you seem thick as thieves. Maybe I'm jealous. Maybe I'm just weak where you're concerned."

The aching she'd felt the night before flared, a monster needing to be fed, nurtured. Damn it, but she didn't need this complication.

"William..." She pushed away from him.

"William can damned well wait," Seth said, drawing her back into his arms. "He's been well paid, fed and more than compensated for having to sleep alone in a nice, big bed instead of on the floor. He's in the car, but he's on the clock."

Charlie felt a twinge of guilt for Seth's reference to the previous night's sleeping arrangements, and she braced herself for the next kiss, but she wasn't prepared, not by a long shot. What was he trying to do? Undermine her emotional stability, divert her capacity to think like a cop, weaken her defenses against him...what? Couldn't the man tell she was already shaken?

"Oh!" she cried. "Please, no more. Like you say, we have a lot to do today."

He looked at her coolly, but she could see the embers of desire still smoldering in his eyes. She may have been granted a reprieve, but he obviously had intentions to finish the discussion they'd started the night before, and when it happened, it'd most likely be on his terms instead of hers.

SETH HANDED the hotel manager Marjorie's photo, half-expecting him to shake his head and deny remembering anything, so Seth was surprised that not only did the man remember her, he had held some of her things she'd never returned to collect.

"What are the odds?" mused Charlie. Even she appeared shocked.

Seth was glad he'd convinced her to spend another night in Guadalajara. Maybe something in the sealed box of clothing and papers contained information that could help both of them. Seth with learning more about his true identity, Charlie with the Martin case.

He'd been reluctant to press her for details. Instinct told him she couldn't, and wouldn't, divulge privileged information, but he was curious to know about Martin and why the case had managed to get under her skin. Seth had a feeling Charlie hadn't had many cases she couldn't solve and that her pride was more on the line than her job should she not succeed.

While they waited for Lawson's things, a wave of nausea hit him, and Seth turned quickly to avoid having Charlie notice. He blinked against the sudden bright light and the ringing in his ears.

What light? he asked himself. *No light when your eyes are closed.* He rubbed his fingertips against his temples and tried steadying his breathing... In, out, more deeply each time... *Slow it down, start, stop, you are in charge, even of your breathing.*

When he opened his eyes, he saw Charlie standing at the hotel registration desk studying a pamphlet left on the counter, and for a moment it was as if they were elsewhere. Houston.

He frowned. He pictured her in tight, skinny jeans and a pair of dingo boots, a soft cowl-neck sweater covering her torso. She was laughing, stopping to smell flowers a Mexican woman proffered.

Seth blinked again. No, the image was still there. *I must be remembering something.* He had no problem differentiating between the Charlie in Houston and the one in Mexico—it wasn't as if he was blending the two images into one. He smiled as he realized he was simply recalling something, a happy time with her.

She replaced the pamphlet then turned and looked into his eyes—her own were troubled, but for a moment he caught the glimmer of something he recognized. Longing. He'd seen that look, right after they'd made love the first time, then gone to a street festival, inside the Loop.

"What?" she asked, walking toward him.

"I think I remembered something," he said reflexively, not meaning to draw her into his thoughts just yet. "The Loop. It's the six-ten highway loop, right?"

She smiled. "Yeah. What made you think of that?"

He shook his head. "I'm still working on it."

The hotel manager returned and placed a medium-sized cardboard box on the desk between him and them. "These are things left in the room. One of the bellboys is bringing 'round the luggage. He had to dust it off where something had spilled on it."

Charlie glanced at Seth sharply, and he knew what she was thinking. Something had spilled. What if it had been evidence of some sort, something that had

DNA? He brushed aside the thought. Whatever had spilled was most likely something recent, something one of the hotel workers had inadvertently dropped back in storage. Too late now anyway. Whoever had the luggage had probably wiped it clean and would be there any second.

Seth motioned toward the box. "I'll get that—just leave it there until the luggage arrives. It most likely has a pull so you won't have a bulky suitcase to carry. Think we can manage?"

She nodded. "Sure."

THE TRUTH. Charlie stretched and clasped her hands behind her neck, cradling her head against her palms. She and Seth had been pouring over the same photos and papers for nearly two hours, and she didn't feel any closer to solving Martin's murder or getting a grip on Lawson's than she had before she arrived in Guadalajara.

The storms had completely passed, leaving in their wake an eerie calm, with soft rain drizzling in fat droplets that barely made a sound on their open window. Seth stood at the open doorway with his back turned to her, his shoulders squared, hips tucked, like a general surveying a battlefield.

She'd struggled to remain calm when he'd remembered something as trivial as the Loop. Didn't mean he remembered her. Just meant his mind was allocating fragmented memories to certain quadrants of his brain, pigeonholing bits of information in case he needed or wanted them later. She wished he'd wanted her badly enough to recall times with her. Maybe he did and wasn't telling her.

Charlie stifled an indelicate snort. Wouldn't that be a convenient way of ditching a relationship that no longer worked? But it had, damn it.

She still couldn't keep from comparing mental notes, that both Martin and Seth had something in common…Mexico. What was here that drew both men? Business? Pleasure? A combination of both?

Wanda Schoonover had been adamant about George Martin's reluctance to travel that day to Mexico, almost as if he was afraid of what might happen. He was supposed to have met with a party at the airport to give him his business information, since his boss, Damien Rogers, was out of the office that week. Rogers, however, had said that all Martin was picking up was his assignment and that the woman who had hired him as an escort had disappeared. That's where the real confusion began. If the police and doctors felt Seth had been riding in the car with Lawson, where did that leave Martin? Could Seth have been sent to replace him with Lawson?

"You're sure you don't remember anything other than her face?" she called.

Seth turned to face her, leaned against the doorjamb and stuffed his hands into his pockets. "No. Wish I did."

"How about the shots Heather took for me of the men at the restaurant?" she asked hopefully.

He indicated the strewn papers on the table before

her. "We've gone over everything at least twice—there's nothing in there about me. Not much about her, for that matter."

Charlie swallowed her disappointment. "Then we're at a dead end. There's no place to go from here except back to Houston."

His face was unreadable, but his eyes held disappointment. "You want to get home that badly?"

Charlie shrugged. "Might as well, unless you can think of a reason to stay." She bit her lip and turned back to face the table, aware of how provocative her words had sounded, even to her own ears. That wasn't where she'd meant to go with him, not at this stage. He'd already turned her down once—she wasn't about to try twice.

She felt more than heard him move away from the door, and her heart beat faster as he approached. The table was a mess, with the paperwork in no specific order, photos of his own accident displayed in a montage with copies of Lawson's and Martin's head shots, their own police reports, crime photos, records of phone calls from Lawson to no-name cell phones, the photos Heather had taken, a disarray of sticky notes… It was all a blur.

Then he touched her. His hands rested gently on her shoulders, his thumbs at the back of her neck, gently pressing, massaging. The fingers on her collarbone. Did she feel them tremble slightly? She didn't dare look over her shoulder, less out of fear for what she'd see in his eyes than what he'd observe in hers. Her quandary, her damned insecurity, her need.

The pressure he exerted intensified slightly, and soon she couldn't help but tilt her head in the opposite direction when she felt his breath against one side of her neck. Closing her eyes, she remembered, even if he couldn't. She inhaled the musky maleness, the air as it softly escaped his nostrils, and her pulse jumped when she detected that he was as deep into the mist as she, that he wanted her, regardless of his doubts.

It happened so fast that she wasn't aware of leaving her seat, of turning to face him. His arms were about her in a flash, lifting her, holding her, his head bending as his lips parted.

Charlie's legs felt shaky, too limp to support her, and her arms were weak, barely able to cling to him as he devoured her, his breath mingling with hers, his lips setting hers afire with a blistering kiss that consumed all rational thought.

Groaning, he clutched her, his hands fisting at the base of her spine, pressing her into him, leaving no doubt as to his body's craving. The thrill of feeling Seth's hard heat burning her, his entire being melding with hers, was her undoing.

She didn't care what happened at this point, as long as he didn't stop kissing her. She didn't care if he remembered her or not, as long as he held her like this, as if his desire for her was a never-ending well of want and need.

This time when he kissed her, she asked no questions, didn't want to know, was too far gone. His touch was bliss, lifting her, carrying her, cradling her, protecting her. For once, her inquisitive mind took a backseat to her heart, and she ran with the unknown, the undiscovered. The Seth she knew no longer existed, and in his place was an exciting stranger.

He picked her up and carried her to his room, settling her on the bed while continuing to kiss and caress her. His hands cupped her bottom and held her in place, and his mouth moved from her lips to her throat, her breasts. He lifted her shirt and bent to suckle her through the flimsy lace and silk of her bra. Charlie moaned and squirmed, unable to hold still. Her own hands fumbled with his zipper.

"I've wanted you for so long," he whispered against her mouth. He kissed her again, leaving her breathless, and then he spent what seemed like hours of bliss nibbling her throat, breasts and stomach. When he moved to kiss between her thighs, she struggled for clarity, fearing that it wouldn't be long before she wouldn't care what he did.

"What about…?" She hesitated to shatter the moment, but safe sex demanded they pause.

He grinned and fished out two foil packets she recognized from the motel's complimentary condom basket in the bathroom.

Charlie giggled and helped him rip open one of the packets. She couldn't speak, could only nod and kiss every place of his body that came near her mouth as he moved above her, stripping them both of the remainder of clothing that separated their bodies.

She'd held out, waited, hoping he'd want her, afraid to encourage him, much less rush him, and now she couldn't wait to feel his body moving inside her, his skin pressed against hers, his hips thrusting in tandem with hers.

Seth didn't disappoint. His fingers probed gently but urgently, opening her, readying her, preparing her for his entrance, and once he settled into her, he closed his eyes, a deep growl escaping his lips. His shoulders tensed beneath her fingers, and the movement of corded muscles throbbing with unleashed rigidity was her undoing. Charlie became liquid heat, a raging fire exploding all around him, uncontained, and she felt as if she'd burn forever.

She rocketed, feeling his hands gripping her, his energy joining with hers, transforming, transcending, their combined fury surpassing anything she'd ever felt.

Both of them shook with spasms, quivering with release then aftermath, and Charlie clung to Seth as shockwaves evaporated into blissful mists, cushioning and comforting her, rocking her gently back to earth.

Seth kissed her sweetly then rolled onto his back, taking her with him.

She wrapped one arm about his waist and snuggled as he stroked her back. This wasn't as she remembered—it was better.

Seth kissed the tip of her nose. "Now aren't you glad we stayed over another night?"

In answer, she threaded her fingers through his hair, bringing his face closer to hers, and she wet her lips. "What do you think?"

He grinned. "Don't suppose you'd mind waiting a second or two? A man can only do so much, you know, without..."

She leaned forward and nibbled his bottom lip, her hand snaking between them to grasp him where he surely least expected it. "I can't wait. I want you now, Seth."

He sputtered for a moment, and when he recovered, he feigned resistance, acting like she was forcing him to do something he despised.

"Nag, nag, nag." He dove under the covers, kissing her breasts, stomach and inner thighs.

CHAPTER EIGHT

HER PARTNER CALLED HER cell phone while she and Seth were at the airport the next day to say he'd run the license plate on the car at the restaurant. "It's a rental," he told Charlie. "Nearly took an act of God to track 'em, but they're Feds."

Charlie had suspected as much.

"Vargas? There's more." Julio sounded concerned.

Damn. "What?" she asked.

"Pretty sure that guy you're with in Mexico was one of Damien Rogers's employees, an escort."

Charlie wasn't surprised, but the news didn't sit well with her. *Why can't I have a normal relationship with a man?* "Let's have it."

"Rogers showed up here yesterday."

"At the precinct?" Charlie was shocked, so much that she had to lower her voice.

"Yep. He came to talk about Martin, to see if we had any leads, and your file on the guy wasn't in the records department, so I checked your station. You had your boyfriend's picture inside your desk, right?"

Charlie almost corrected him to say that Seth

wasn't her boyfriend, but she kept mum on the subject and simply asked him to continue.

"So I'm looking for that file, and there was that picture of your boyfriend sitting in a drawer, and when I opened it, with him peering over my shoulder, it was like this man Rogers had seen a ghost or something. He stared and stared then said he thinks this guy worked for him, too, but he couldn't recall his name. You had it listed on the back of the picture, so I gave it to him. He started nodding, said yep, that was him, said the guy just disappeared one day and he never heard from him again."

Julio kept rambling. "I call bullshit on that one. Two men who work for him disappear, and he doesn't know what happened to either of them? Either the escort business has a high turnover rate, or this guy's dirty, Vargas."

Charlie set her jaw grimly. *And Seth is involved.* "Anything else?"

"Yeah, the Feds were here as well, checking on a guy named Mason Aldridge and asking what you were doing in Mexico."

"What?" This time Charlie couldn't repress a small shriek.

"Seems they sent an agent to Mexico to attend some function because Aldridge was in cahoots with somebody importing illegal aliens across the border, something related to terrorism. I didn't catch all of it because once Bemo had them in his office, they shut the door and drew the blinds." Julio paused. "Who is Aldridge? Only reference I found to him was that he was listed in an accident report along with one Marjorie Lawson—you had a copy of that on your desk, too. That happened out of our jurisdiction. We investigating that as well? That what you're doing in Mexico?"

When she didn't respond, Julio added, "Sorry. Didn't mean to snoop, just thought I could help."

"No. Hang on a sec." Charlie felt sick to her stomach. She glanced up to see Seth from across the room, his eyes intent upon her features. She was sure she must've looked guilty at first because her first thoughts were that Seth had to have been involved with Aldridge to have been linked to him, to have Aldridge's sister so quick to have Seth's features altered to resemble those of her brother.

Was she to spend the next hour on a plane sitting beside someone with whom she'd just made love, knowing he might be a man possibly involved in terrorism? The thought boggled her mind. And why were the Feds investigating her? Because she was with Seth?

She cleared her throat and scrambled to find a plausible response to Julio's questions. "The Aldridge and Lawson cases aren't ours—I was helping out a friend." *Think fast, Charlie, think.* "Something made me wonder if their accident was somehow related to George Martin's murder, considering the time frame—Lawson was killed not long after Martin was supposed to fly to Mexico, Guadalajara to be precise. Can't figure it out, though, so by all means, knock yourself out."

That seemed to satisfy Rodríguez, but his call triggered a reminder of something that had been needling her.

"Julio, do me a favor?"

"Sure. Shoot."

Charlie gave him the name of the doctor in California who had presided over the majority of Seth's surgeries. "Find out who paid Mason's bills if you can. I'm interested to see if it was the sister."

"What does he have to do with any of this?" Charlie considered her words. "It's complicated. I'd rather have concrete proof if you can get it."

He agreed then updated her on a couple of other things and rang off, telling her he had a lunch date.

Charlie was stunned. First Rogers, then the Feds checking on Seth? Well, on him and Aldridge. *Now me? What are the odds? We all have to be linked. What is the one thing or person that links us? George Martin?*

She covered her face with her hands, letting her fingers massage her temples. She could handle the disappointment if Seth was involved with Marjorie Lawson—it'd hurt, but she'd survive. She couldn't honestly say the same if he was a party to murder. What had he done to warrant federal involvement? And what had she done, other than love a man with no memory?

Charlie gave herself a mental shake. He hadn't

done anything—neither had she. Aldridge and Lawson were American citizens. It made sense that the CIA would be involved, no matter who was at fault.

It was the terrorist theory that worried her.

She lifted her head from her hands and flipped the switch from distraught female to savvy detective. Scrutinizing Seth from hairline to shoe heels, she monitored his gait, sure and steady, his hands as they hung by his sides without clenching, his eyes, focused yet quickly darting when a sudden movement captured his attention. A baby lifting a rattle to shake in the air, a woman crossing her legs, a man catching his cap as it fell from his head. Seth noticed it all, unobtrusively unless a trained cop had him in her sights.

He was too alert, not laid back enough, to be a mere escort. The man exuded sex appeal, sure, but Seth was nobody's boy to be bossed about and told how to dress or where to go. She couldn't see him as an escort, which left…

"CIA?" SETH LOOKED from one man to the other. They'd been at the gate when he and Charlie had left the ramp in Houston. Seth's first impulse upon seeing them, especially the taller one, had been to fight. To reach for the nearest object that could separate the man's head from his shoulders.

"Whoa!" When the shorter of them held up his hands and cautioned his partner to back off, he reminded the taller guy, "He's had a head injury, remember? But he's still one of us. Give him a few moments to get his bearings."

Seth shook his head. "I'm CIA?"

The taller man, Runnels, nodded and put the gun he'd drawn away, but something about him set Seth's nerves on edge. Runnels' expression changed from one of cold calculation to wary sympathy. "You don't remember me?"

"Not really." Seth looked from Runnels to Stone. "I worked with both of you?"

Stone patted him on the shoulder, and his eyes seemed genuinely sad. "It'll come back to you, Seth."

Charlie had remained silent during the encounter, and when the news he'd finally absorbed had settled, Seth reached out to hold her hand. The action raised eyebrows on both Stone and Runnels. Charlie, on the other hand, didn't so much as flinch. Her hand felt clammy rather than her usual warm temperature. Her posture alarmed him as well. She stood ramrod straight as if someone had a knife pressing against her.

He couldn't resist releasing her hand and touching the small of her back. The muscles just above the waistband of her trousers tensed, and he knew she was upset, but he wasn't sure why. He figured she'd be glad he'd finally discovered who he was.

"Guess you'd better cowboy up," she said, moving away from his touch. "I'm sure these men have a lot to discuss with you."

"Actually, with both of you, ma'am." Runnels gave her an apologetic but firm look. "Our car is parked out front."

This time it was Charlie who lifted an eyebrow. "Aren't you afraid of getting a ticket by one of Houston's finest?"

Runnels touched his jacket that hid his badge. "Not with one of these." He motioned for them to follow them out of the airport.

The trip from their gate to the parked car, which had yet another suit as sentry, was short. The man waiting with the car tossed a set of keys to Stone, gave a small salute and turned on his heel.

"Another of ours who was in the neighborhood," explained Runnels. "He has to board a plane for Borneo, so we gave him a lift."

"Where are we going?" Charlie asked, once she and Seth were settled in the backseat of the Lincoln. She touched the leather upholstery, her fingers trailing close to Seth's leg, but when he reached for her hand she snatched it away and smoothed her slacks.

The two Feds exchanged a quick look but refrained from answering.

"Okay." Her voice was low and dripped sarcasm.

Runnels sighed. "There are some things we need to discuss with both of you in our office. It'll keep until we're there, and we're only a few minutes away."

Most likely my last assignment, thought Seth. *They probably want to ask me about my last memo-*

ries, what I remember if anything, what really happened in Mexico. As if I know. He studied the backs of the men before them, the shapes of their heads, their necks, hands, shoulders. Was he like them? Staid, stoic, so straight-laced they sat like they had sticks up their asses?

Seth glanced at Charlie, who was still silent as a tomb, as if she was still taking all of it in and processing it. *Welcome to my world.* He hadn't told her about the flashes he'd been getting, not exactly full-blown memories, but snapshots from a photo album whose story didn't make sense. A face, a scent, a voice or a name. The memories were coming in piece by piece, much like he imagined the car accident he was in. Swift, in actuality, but demonically slow as his mind's projector ran the movie.

He hoped something at the CIA office would unlock a few more doors in his memory bank.

That memory bank should have remained locked. Forever. Seth sat, stunned, silent, listening as Stone and Runnels explained, in front of Charlie, that she had been his mark, his assignment.

At first, Charlie had gasped, and Seth had caught the shimmer of tears in her eyes before she'd turned from them, from him, to stare out of the fifth-floor windows. He could see the rapid rise and fall of her ribcage as she struggled to leash the rage he was sure was building.

He almost felt sorry for Runnels and Stone as they

paused uncomfortably, allowing Charlie and Seth to register the news.

"The police had jurisdiction over the dating service until our guy got killed, but we weren't ready to let anyone know Martin was ours." Stone drummed his fingertips against the desk between him and Runnels and Seth and Charlie. He turned to address Charlie. "We let the police think what they wanted, do their investigation, draw their own conclusions, but we had Seth buddy up to you to see what information your department had on Martin's disappearance."

"Wouldn't it have made better sense to simply ask us?" She set her jaw, and her eyes glistened.

Runnels shrugged. "Probably, but the powers that be wanted everything kept covert a while longer." He indicated Seth. "Then he got himself lost."

"I wasn't lost," Seth seethed. "I was comatose."

"You were still out of play, my friend." Stone's tone was gentle.

"I was really important to all of you, wasn't I, friend?" Sarcasm laced the last syllable of Seth's sentence. "That why it took you so long to contact me?"

Stone looked sad for a moment. "We were under orders to see how much you'd find out if you believed you were Mason Aldridge."

So I was just supposed to get close to Charlie in the beginning. Not fall in love with her, Seth pondered. Damn it. How could he have been so callous as to have used her to find out more about the Martin case? How could he, as a professional, have allowed himself to fall in love with her?

He knew instantly—it would have been more than difficult. It would have been impossible to have spent time with Charlie and not fallen for her.

"So that's why he remembered my phone number," Charlie mused from her stance at the window.

"No," Seth disagreed. "It was more than that."

She whirled, unmindful, or so it seemed at first, of the agents in the room with them. "Really? How do you know? How will we ever know for sure?" She cast a scornful glance at Stone and Runnels. "At least they've cleared up a few things, like why me, why Mexico—it was because Martin was one of them, one of you…whatever you are. Spies?" Charlie snorted. "So are you all like double-o-seven types who travel to foreign countries in search of evil?"

"It's not like that, ma'am," said Stone.

Charlie shook a finger at him. "I am not your mother—I'm a police officer. You call me ma'am one more time instead of Detective Vargas, and I'll shove my badge so far down your throat it'll take a proctologist to find it."

She glared at Seth. "What? Detective Vargas doesn't work for you? It's not like I was more than a job, right?" Then she seemed to be thinking. "Did Bemo know about this?"

The two Feds looked guilty. Stone finally nodded.

"He knew. We had to ask him to keep it from you, though."

The look on her face said it all, her shock and dismay. "How long has he known?" demanded Charlie. "Not that it matters in the scheme of things, but I'd like to know just how long I was under a federal microscope with my boss's knowledge."

"Not until you were in Mexico," Runnels told her. "We'd figured out Seth might be regaining his memory, and when we saw that you were traveling with him, we had to know what the two of you were doing in Guadalajara. If he'd blown his cover, it would have been disastrous for the bureau."

"Great." Charlie nodded. "Thanks. Sincerely." She cut Seth another hard look. "Information at last."

Seth took a long, shuddering breath. He detected no sarcasm, despite the words. What he heard and felt were deep-seated pain and disappointment in Charlie's voice. This had to be killing her, especially after they'd made love right before coming home. He felt like an ass, but there was nothing he could say or do that would make any difference to her now. Even if he regained full memory and tried convincing her that he'd loved her all along, she'd never believe him, not after today.

Stone walked behind his desk and pulled out a sheaf of papers, rifling through them then dividing them and passing half to Seth. "I hope our revelation won't affect the job we need the two of you to perform."

Charlie glanced from one man to the other. “What? Now I have to work with him?”

Stone handed Charlie the other half of the paper-work. “We need the two of you to continue as if you were a couple, to be seen, to chat up certain things, to draw the man we suspect of murdering Martin into the open.”

Charlie shoved the papers back at him. “No, thanks.”

Stone quietly but firmly handed them back to her, tapping her on the chest with them when she didn’t open her hands to receive them. “I’m afraid you don’t have a choice, Detective. We’ve already spoken with your captain, and both departments are working together now to bring this man to justice. He’s murdered two of our agents and nearly killed another.” He indicated Seth. “Surely, you see the importance of your participation.”

“Two?” Seth asked. “Lawson was the other?”

“Right,” said Runnels. “When Martin didn’t show up for their rendezvous in Guadalajara, you were sent. The two of you had attended a stockholders meeting of Aldridge Enterprises and were on your way back to your hotel when you were run off the road, most likely by Mason. We know he was there because of airport security. We believe he followed you, tried to kill you, then came home while you were in the hospital and Lawson was in the morgue.”

Seth rubbed his eyes. “So the Mexican police had

it right all along. That's why I kept seeing Lawson's profile. She was driving."

"Right."

Seth continued. "I'm confused. So who the hell was driving which car?"

Stone chuckled. "I'm not surprised—it's pretty tangled. You were riding with Marjorie, on your way to attend a function at the hotel as our undercover operatives. Dorinda and Doug Wilkerson were in the other car. As for Mason Aldridge, nobody knows where he was at that time."

Runnels sat on the edge of the desk across from Seth. "We're not sure what happened to the real Aldridge, but he was involved with smuggling terrorists into our country via Rogers's business, the escort service. These men and women would enter through customs, travel as far as Houston, where Rogers trained them, then travel to various parts of the country to work with others like them. We don't know how many cells there are, how many escort services Rogers truly owns, or who else is involved, but it's a big operation."

Charlie held up her hands. "Illegal aliens...terrorist transports?"

Stone nodded. "We know you're familiar with a different kind of illegal alien problem, what with the Texas border bumped up against that of Mexico. What we're referring to are illegals from countries other than Mexico. They're being smuggled in from Mexico, transported via the dating service loop."

He shrugged. "Not all of them are being handed off to the dating service, of course, but they are entering the country mixed in with others who are simply here to find work or attend school. Makes those working for the dating service more difficult to catch."

"We've tracked at least two hundred illegal aliens during the past eighteen months, and we're pretty sure they all arrived thanks to Aldridge and Rogers. Some of them, as we said, find jobs, attend college, while others within the same families are recruited to work for the escort service."

Charlie's mouth gaped. "That many?"

Stone nodded. "These men and women working for the dating service must have families, friends, people with whom they relate. Otherwise, they'd be too easy for us to catch. Their governments don't send them over here flying solo. They're given families, backgrounds, loved ones, so that they blend in with our culture."

"Fellas, I'm not sure I'll be much use to you," Seth admitted. "I haven't had a gun in my hands since I've been out of the hospital, and I can't remember much—short-term memory problems more than long-term."

"Doesn't matter," Stone said, coming to join them. "You won't be issued a weapon, not until you pass muster with the powers that be. But you're still technically engaged by the CIA, so you have a job to do, regardless."

Charlie interrupted them. "Whoa. You want us as sitting ducks, don't you? That's what this is about—you've said as much. You need someone to draw Rogers into the open." She waved her arms expressively. "If he's already killed two of your agents, what makes you so certain you can protect us, especially if Seth has no way of defending himself? That's a suicide mission you're feeding us."

Bile rose in Seth's throat. She made him sound like a victim, and regardless of his memory, he was pretty damned sure he'd never been the type to roll over and wait for someone to kill him. "You think I can't defend myself or protect you?" he blurted out.

"Oh, don't get your boxers in a twist," she snapped. "This isn't about ego, it's about self-preservation."

Seth pounded the desk. "Bring it on. I have a lot more at stake here than you realize, babe." Pride be damned, he had Charlie to think about, not just his hide.

"Hold on," Stone said, pushing his palms toward them. "Nobody's asking you to die for the cause, just to be seen in certain circles, to let him get close enough to talk to you. We'd need you to wear a wire, of course, and to pretend Seth is really Aldridge. We need him on tape."

Seth shook his head. "Why didn't whoever manages the escort service approach me before now?"

"Probably for the same reason we didn't—to see how much you really knew."

Seth sighed. "Okay. I get it now. Even though I didn't know shit, neither of you could possibly know that unless you watched me and kept me close."

Charlie squinted and leaned closer, as if examining a bug under a microscope. "I don't know what you've been smoking, but last time I checked, killers don't do a lot of chatting."

Stone folded his arms across his chest and nodded. "I don't suppose it's occurred to you, Detective Vargas…" And he made a point of emphasizing the title she'd thrown at him earlier. "But you're the one Seth can thank for having put him in Rogers's gun sites. You're the reason Seth has a target on him now. If you hadn't gone to Rogers asking so many questions about George Martin…"

"I was working a cold case," Charlie shot back. "I was doing my job!"

"You were nosing around to see what had happened to your boyfriend, Miss Vargas," Stone said, rising and placing his hands on his hips. "You didn't give a damn about George Martin." He held up his hands again, palms facing her. "Not that I believe you don't do your job well, but Martin meant nothing to you." He stuck a thumb in Seth's direction. "My pal over here, however, had gotten under your skin, and you couldn't handle it that he'd simply dropped out of sight. You went back to face Rogers more because of Seth than George. You just wanted to know where your boyfriend was, not who had killed George."

"You think you know me pretty well, don't you?" Her question wasn't defensive, more a statement of surprise.

"I know you better than you'd like, lady. That's what bugs you."

By then, Seth and Runnels had moved toward the center of the room to get between Charlie and Stone, both of whom were red-faced and seemed itching for a verbal brawl.

Seth felt compelled to defend Charlie, even though he knew the little spitfire could handle her own against anyone. He felt torn between the job he couldn't perform and the woman he loved, and the realization that he loved her ate at him like a cancer. He knew in his heart she felt nothing but remorse, anger, bitterness and disappointment that she'd ever become involved with him.

"Knock it off, Stone." Seth stood and moved between the two antagonistic law officers.

"I can take care of myself." Charlie grabbed his arm and pulled him aside. Her lower lip trembled slightly, and she lifted her head proudly, almost defiantly. She swallowed hard enough for him to see a slight movement in her throat, and she wet her lips before facing Stone and continuing. "What is it you need from me? Do I call my captain, or does he know where I am?"

Stone's expression softened, noted Seth, and his voice had a more even, kinder tone. "Bemo knows. We'll need you two to spend a couple of nights in a hotel while we check out your apartment. You don't have any pets, do you?"

When Charlie shook her head, he continued, "We'll sweep the room for bugs, place a couple of our people to watch your building and floor, and install a camera or two so we can see who's watching you."

"But nobody knows where I live," Charlie protested.

Runnels shook his head. "You'd be surprised. If Rogers knew enough to follow you to Mexico—"

Seth's mind snapped to attention. "What?" He and Charlie exchanged disbelieving glances.

He could tell it had slipped the other two men's minds to inform them.

Charlie looked as if her knees were buckling, and she reached for the nearest chair and sat. "Rogers… was in Mexico?"

"He was on your flight." Stone's voice was quiet, matter-of-fact.

Stone opened the door to the small office and quietly asked someone for a few bottles of water to be delivered. Seth felt as if someone had kicked him in the teeth.

When Stone turned back from the door, a flash of recognition, something…it triggered a montage of scenes that flitted across Seth's mind. He and Stone both laughing, doing mundane things like watching television together—a football game, Texas against Oklahoma.

When Runnels turned around and caught Seth's eye, Seth gave a brief nod. "We were all friends?" he asked.

For the first time since they'd all met at the airport, Runnels smiled. "You and I trained together, and you were best man at Stone's wedding."

"How long have you two known one another?" Seth asked, directing his question to Stone.

"We only met a couple of weeks ago," Stone said. "But we've had some good talks about you."

Charlie obtrusively cleared her throat. When they all looked at her, she crossed her legs at the ankles, tucked them under her chair and leaned forward. "Charming as this little reunion has been, I do have a life, family, a job, so can we get through this as quickly as possible so I can go home?"

CHAPTER NINE

THEY HADN'T EVEN LET HER GO home for fresh clothes, telling her and Seth that someone would retrieve their belongings and take them to the hotel. She'd bet her last paycheck Seth didn't have a pile of laundry waiting on him back at his mansion…rather, Aldridge's mansion.

Charlie could barely contain her anger. First he was some rich manufacturing magnate, then her amnesiac lover, possibly a male escort, a CIA operative and now all of the above plus someone who had used her for his own purposes? She'd always admired all aspects of law enforcement, but now she saw an ugly side she had difficulty appreciating. If she was ever in the position of ripping someone from their home, she'd remember this. If she ever had to go undercover and lie to those she loved, she'd think twice before taking on the assignment.

She winced guiltily. As if he had a choice. Still.

Once at the hotel, she checked out her room, noting that they at least were in a large suite, one in which she had her own bedroom. She heard Stone asking Seth what he wanted for the next day's meals since they'd be sequestered, and since the hotel had provided a checklist.

Seth seemed not to hear what was being said—or he was off in la-la land, because he never answered. Charlie moved to stand in her doorway leading to the living area she'd share with Seth, and she watched his face, his eyes. He'd completely spaced out and seemed to have difficulty following the conversation. Stone, whose back was to Seth, had apparently not noticed.

"Hey," she said gently, going to stand beside Seth.

He nodded, but his eyes still seemed unfocused to her, as if he searched for something.

"Did you catch what he said?" Charlie asked.

Stone, upon hearing her, had quit talking and turned to Seth. "Buddy, you okay?"

"I'm fine." Seth brushed aside their concern and flexed. "I'm just tired, sorry. You were asking me something?"

Stone reiterated his questions, seemingly oblivious to what had just happened, but Charlie had a moment of panic. How awful for Seth, if this was part of what he'd mentioned, the short-term memory problems. To be suddenly cut adrift from his thoughts like that, unexpectedly.

She shoved aside her sympathies. *Oh, no, Charlie—uh-uh, he still lied to you by omission. The man used you. Don't get sucked back into anything. Focus on the case, on helping them nab Rogers.*

"Detective?" Runnels handed her a copy of the

same list Stone had been going over with Seth. "We're asking you both to fill these out now so that you won't have to open your doors once we leave. You should be fine, but we'll have a guard posted outside, just in case."

She nodded, accepting the piece of paper and pen he offered. As she sat at her bedroom desk, filling in the squares by checking them, she couldn't help but dwell on Seth, despite her desire not to sympathize. He'd take offense at too much concern, but damn it, she cared. He wasn't an invalid—he wasn't even traumatized. He was simply confused momentarily. It was what was happening in that moment and what occurred afterward that concerned Charlie. How did he feel when he spaced out like that? And was the condition permanent?

When she handed Runnels her selection and he asked if she could think of anything in particular she needed or wanted for the next couple of days, she nodded and gave him the names of a couple of board games and card games.

He lifted an eyebrow. "Okay. I'll see what I can do."

Charlie sat on the edge of her bed. Let the Feds pick up the tab and think she was a little nutty. Maybe playing with games that required memory skills would help Seth. Couldn't hurt, and it'd pass the time. Might keep her mind off thoughts of him kissing and holding her if she had something else on which to concentrate.

Tall order, she thought, but it was worth a shot.

He seemed to have picked up on her scheme. After the others left, he asked her about her requests. "Memory games?"

"Card games," she countered.

"Think you'll be bored, do you?" This time his voice was edgy, less joking.

Charlie spread her hands on the dinette table in their suite. "Let's cut the crap. You have memory issues—I was just trying to help." She watched his features morph from congenial to outright angry.

"Charlie, while I appreciate your concern, butt out."

"Pardon me?"

"I don't want your sympathy, and there's nothing you could do about my situation anyway. I've been to the best doctors, and they all say the same thing—that I can get shunts put into my skull to drain some of the fluid, but the memory loss is most likely permanent."

The anger she'd felt disintegrated. "Seth, I don't feel sorry for you."

"Yeah?" He pierced her with a steely blue stare. "What do you feel, Charlie?"

Her name, soft on his lips, was her undoing. She rose and went to him. He was stiff at first, his arms hanging at his sides, his chest expanding with every breath.

"It's only a hug, Seth, not a contract." She pressed herself against him.

"Like I'd hate a contract with you, emotional or otherwise." Finally his arms wrapped around her, squeezing her gently, letting her know how much her presence meant to him.

Charlie couldn't have remained angry if she'd tried. "Why didn't you tell me how bad your injuries were?" she asked.

Seth released her and held her at arm's length. "I had my face rearranged, a new one sewn onto my skull, and got my cage rattled, my brains loosened. I walked away from it, so what else is there to say?"

She led him to the couch but didn't sit when he did. "Want some coffee?"

"Sure." He lifted an eyebrow. "Don't suppose you cook, too, do you?"

She grinned. "No, but I'm great at dialing room service. Give me a couple of minutes and I'll have some food sent up." She stuck a thumb in the direction of the hall outside their door. "Of course, Agent Double-O-Eight, or someone not as far up the CIA echelon as you and your buddies, will probably have to run their fingers over it to check for sugar bombs or veggie arsenic."

He smiled in return. "This mean you'll keep me company and talk to me so we can work this out?"

Charlie shrugged. "Nothing to work out. You had a job to do, so did I."

"Yeah, but you weren't assigned to follow me, get close to me, so whatever happened between us can't be suspect because of your actions."

She didn't say anything. Whatever came out of her mouth wouldn't make him feel better anyway, so she opted for silence while she found the number she needed and punched the buttons on the telephone.

She'd no sooner hung up the hotel phone than her cell phone rang—it was her father.

"You okay?" he asked.

"I'm fine."

"Mind telling me where you are and what the hell these two men are doing in your apartment?"

Charlie blinked. "What?"

"These two yahoos sitting in the middle of your living room floor. Who are they?"

"Dad? Why are they—did you hurt them?"

Sam sighed dramatically. "One of them has a headache and the other a sore jaw. You know that lamp near your front door? I'll buy you a new one. I never liked that lamp anyway."

Charlie chuckled. At least he wasn't the one hurting. "What happened?"

"Forget what happened here. Where are you?"

Charlie gave Sam a condensed version of what had happened since she'd gotten off the plane in Houston. "I'm sorry I didn't call. Things have been moving kinda fast, and I completely forgot."

"Yeah, well I didn't. Knew when you were supposed to get back, and you didn't call, so I picked up some beer and a bouquet of flowers and thought I'd surprise you." He snorted. "Guess I wasn't the only one who got surprised."

"You bought me flowers? Aw, Daddy!"

"They were five bucks at the store where I bought the beer," he said, brushing aside her gushing. Then he swore. "Damn. I forgot to pick up something for my cell phone. My charger in the car is goin' out on me."

She asked again what had happened.

"I start to knock, see the door is open, walk in, and I ask the first guy if he's Seth. He said no, so I clocked him on the jaw. The other guy comes at me, so I pick up the lamp and throw it at him." Sam paused. "Once they started comin' around, I asked them who they were, and they told me their badges were in their jackets. Figured I'd better call you to confirm."

"So why are they sitting on the floor of my living room?" she asked indulgently.

"Because I haven't untied them yet. Thank God you don't always hang up your clothes—your bathrobe and nightgown were lying over the arm of the couch. And before you get all pissed off, I had to do something before they woke up. I'm an old man—they're bigger than I am."

At that, Charlie laughed. Sam was anything but helpless, but she could see his point.

"Look, Dad, I'll explain everything else when I see you."

"And when will that be? Charlene, you're not getting off the damned hook here, so you'd better start talking." Now he sounded upset, and she couldn't blame him.

"Seth is one of them, CIA, and right now we're in a hotel." She gave him the address. "But I doubt they'll let you in here."

Sam snorted again. "They'll let me in, or I'll raise so much hell their boss in D.C. will hear me."

He seemed to have turned from the phone a second. Charlie could hear him complaining in the background to one of the men on the floor. "Oh, shut up. I didn't hit you that hard. I'm talkin' here to my daughter—I'll be with you in a second."

She stifled a giggle and told him she loved him. "I have to check in with my partner," she told him.

"Oh, you don't call your old man, but you'll call your partner? I see how you are."

Charlie started to retort that it must've been a trick she'd learned from him, because she'd heard her mom complain often enough about how Sam would cover every base but home if he had the chance.

"I'll talk to you again tomorrow, okay?" she said instead.

Sam's voice was gruff. "I love you, Charlene. Watch your ass."

He wasn't exactly the type of father to make chicken soup or take his daughter to the ballet, but then she wasn't the chicken soup and ballet type daughter. Besides, his heart was in the right place.

She felt her cheeks grow pink. And he'd bought her flowers. How sweet.

When she hung up, she caught Seth watching her. Suddenly her throat went dry. The look in his eyes was dark, brooding.

"What are you thinking?" she asked.

"Of you." His eyes held wonder, confusion, pain and something she couldn't identify. "I wonder what it is you ever saw in me, but I have no problem with what I see in you."

Charlie felt buoyed and deflated all at once. What did she say to something like that? He wasn't angling for a compliment. He was giving one. "You became my best friend," she finally said, finding her voice. "I could tell you things I couldn't tell anyone else." She swallowed before continuing. "Of course, at the time I didn't realize that your job was to get me to reveal what I thought and did."

The tender thread of intimacy between them began to unravel.

He raised his head as if stretching his neck muscles and closed his eyes. "Somehow, I don't think that's all we had going for us." He relaxed, opened his eyes and leveled his gaze upon her again. "Do you?"

Honesty was stronger than pride. She shook her head. "No." She moved toward the couch where he still sat. "We had a lot more than that."

He patted a place beside him. She'd rather have crawled into his lap, but she sat next to him then turned to face him, crossing her legs and propping her elbows on her knees, studying him.

"You want to know what we talked about?" she asked.

"Please." His relief was visible, tenuous.

She smiled and sat back, leaning against a cushion. "We discussed places we'd been. I remember you telling me about Singapore, Taiwan, Bangkok, cities where you'd traveled. We never discussed our jobs—that was something neither of us was eager to get into, but we talked about facets of our work, and yours involved a lot of travel."

He shook his head. "Weird thing is that I can tell you right now about streets in those cities, but I couldn't tell you why I was there."

"But you're remembering something. Maybe that's a sign that your memories are coming back," she said hopefully.

"What else did we talk about?"

Charlie thought a moment. "Family. I was an only child—you were, too. You talked about your aunt in Louisiana and how she raised you after your parents died." She paused and gauged his reaction. He hadn't told her much, but he'd mentioned the aunt in passing.

Seth didn't seem sad. Quite the contrary—it was as if a veil had been lifted. "Aunt Patricia. Everyone called her Patty. She was my father's sister." His face brightened, and he guffawed. "I'll be damned.

Of course." His voice grew excited. "I can see her house, a big two-story on Magnolia."

He looked at her in surprise. For a moment, Charlie thought he was going to kiss her. His hands grasped her shoulders, and she felt his excitement running through both of them. Then, it was as if a large wave of reality washed over him, and he dropped his grip on her.

Charlie waited, knowing he'd remembered something else.

"She died," he finally said, "about two years after I got out of training. I was in China at the time and couldn't make it back in time for her funeral. She knew she was going and had left instructions with her attorney that I most likely couldn't be reached until after she was laid to rest."

Seth groaned. "God, why now? Why couldn't I have remembered this crap right after the accident? It would have saved us so much time."

Charlie leaned forward, clasped his hands and drew them to her lap. "There's nothing you could have done in Mexico, Seth. I was in Houston, and you were stuck there for a long while. What's past is just that… It can't be relived."

He nodded and clenched her hands, circling his thumbs over the insides of her wrists. "I guess what's bugging me now is that so much has happened that was out of my control, and I hope I haven't completely destroyed whatever you once felt for me." He tugged on her hands and brought her closer.

Charlie's heart skipped a beat. At last. She was tired of carrying a grudge. It was time to put the past completely behind them and work on what they could salvage today.

Seth brushed his lips against hers. "I'm sorry, Charlie, for everything. For being a lying, conniving, secretive jerk who used you, even if it was my job. I should have come clean with you or bowed out of the assignment, something, as soon as I realized I was falling for you—and I'm sure that I did."

She kissed him back, practically throwing herself into his lap. "Why do you say that?"

"Because I'm falling for you now. And while it feels like the first time, I know that it's not, because it feels too familiar." His lips claimed hers once again, and this time the pressure he exerted was stronger, more demanding. His hands left hers and held her head, lovingly, tenderly, with an excruciating gentleness that left her breathless.

Just when she felt she'd melt completely, a loud thumping on the door alerted her that their food had arrived. Damn it.

She disengaged long enough to stare into his eyes before answering the door. "Hold that thought."

SETH MOANED SOFTLY when she left to collect their food. He didn't know if he could suffer more unrequited arousal without exploding. Every time she was near him, every time he looked at her, he felt himself harden with a heat that threatened to combust. And damned if they weren't always interrupted by either growling stomachs from lack of food or from food itself making an appearance at an inopportune moment. Maybe it was a sign that one of them needed to become a chef. Forget the cops and robbers stuff, nix the spy games and concentrate on culinary arts.

He watched as she set everything on the coffee table, arranging who got what and making room for their drinks. Somehow seeing Charlie in a domestic mode soothed a side of him he hadn't known existed. He wanted more of this calm domesticity, but that in and of itself was disturbing. Both of them were career law enforcement.

Well, she was. Didn't appear he'd have much to offer to the job if he couldn't pull himself together without his memory screwing him. Remembering his childhood or a city he'd visited was one thing. Recalling minutia, details pertinent to an assignment? That was a whole new ballgame, one in which he wasn't sure he could play.

As Charlie settled beside him, Seth thought of what had just happened between them. It wasn't fair of him to saddle her with a man so unlike the one he'd been before the accident. Not that he was some invalid who had to be babysat, but he was hardly the same person. He swallowed his disappointment. She deserved better. Someone who could talk shop, understand her job and what she went through on a daily basis, share the ups and downs of police work, and both commiserate and brainstorm with her. Would she be as effective if she was worried about him?

He hated doing so, but he broke the mood before she could pick up where they'd left off. He asked about the phone call she'd just received.

"Your dad, I take it, was on the phone earlier?"

"Huh? Oh, yeah." She smiled. "Seems he bought me flowers." She laughed while spearing a bite to eat with her fork. "It's been so long since a man gave me flowers, I hardly knew what to say to him. Didn't want to make too big a deal about it because it would've embarrassed him. But it was sweet." Then she covered her mouth with her napkin and shook her head. "Not that I was implying anything. I mean, I wasn't hinting."

He reassured her he was fine with the subject. "I take it I never gave you flowers?"

She shook her head. "That's not important. It's that he did this. Sam isn't the hearts and flowers type." She chuckled. "He also bought beer if that tells you anything. What father takes his daughter daisies and beer?"

"What makes you think they're daisies?"

She blushed. "Because I used to love them when I was a kid. Those and carnations."

Charlie continued talking between bites. "My father and I play this 'what if' game when I'm on a case. He's retired from the force, and he puts me through all these scenarios, taking me from one idea to another until I finally get where I'm meant to go. I think Sam always wanted a boy, but he got me instead."

"I'm sure that's not the case," Seth said.

"Probably a little of both," she confessed, "but I'm okay with it. So is he, especially since I turned out to be so much like him. It's one more thing he can secretly lord over my mother, who pretty much loathes the man. He's just happy to be out of the relationship with her, while Mom hangs onto the past like it's her favorite winter coat she can't give up, no matter how ratty and worn it is."

Suddenly she narrowed her eyes and squinted at him. "Why this conversation? You get cold feet while I was collecting this stuff at the door?" She indicated the food on the coffee table.

Seth shrugged. "Don't get me wrong. I'm not sorry we went there. I just realized that I'm being unfair to you."

"How so?" She put her fork down and wiped her lips again.

Although it pained him, Seth tried putting things into perspective for her. "I'm no longer the man you met last year. I'm not sure about a lot of things—you're the only thing that even makes sense to me anymore."

She seemed impatient. She set her jaw and nodded, but he didn't get the feeling she agreed with a damn thing he said, just that she wanted him to get to the point.

"Charlie, like I said before, I hope I haven't destroyed what we had." He took a deep breath. "I hope we can at least remain friends. Good friends."

He may as well have slapped her, if her expression was any indication. Seth immediately regretted having said anything at all.

"Friends?" She tossed her napkin onto the table. "You want to be my friend? As in going to movies or maybe even having a beer with me and my dad? Or maybe you thought we'd be weekend bed and bath buddies now and then but not live together?"

"That's not what I meant at all," he tried explaining.

But it was too late. He could tell he'd done more than just piss her off this time. She was hurt, and there was absolutely nothing he could do about it at this point.

LIFE AS SHE'D known it had never been so all-consuming and complicated since she'd met Seth Taggart. School, then the academy, life on the force, time with her mom and dad, albeit separately. Life had been the job, the occasional after-hours drink with one of her coworkers, a day off now and then. But never the emotional upheaval she'd experienced since meeting and falling in love with Seth.

Charlie tossed and turned all night, unable to sleep peacefully, unable to simply rest when she was awake and staring at the ceiling. She didn't even have a problem admitting to herself that she was in love with him. Of course, she hadn't let him know she felt the same now as she had the previous year. For one thing, there hadn't been time. For another, whenever it seemed the appropriate moment to discuss or show him, there had been one interruption after another. Now this. Was he crazy or was she? Didn't he know she didn't give a damn what obstacles they'd have to overcome as long as they could be together? Or was that not enough for him? How could they go on like this, living on what-ifs and maybes? It wasn't fair to either of them, and perhaps that was what he'd been thinking when he'd suggested they be friends.

She looked at the clock beside the bed and groaned. She was of a mind to march into his bedroom and tell him off, let him know just where he could shove his self-sacrificing suggestion. At least one of them would feel better. Might as well be her.

What little rationality she had left surfaced, though, and the mindset that had gotten her through the academy and every case she'd worked on afterward took hold. No, she'd see this Martin case through to the end, especially now that she knew how it connected to Seth. Maybe with closure on his coworkers' deaths he could move forward, see that it didn't matter where he worked or that they'd both have to contend with the fallout should he not recover the rest of his memory.

When the sun rose, she'd be dressed and ready to roll, tell Stone and Runnels she had no intention of staying another night in a hotel when she could be in the comfort of her own home, small as it was. She'd manage to escape them all for a while, gather the rest of her information with Julio's help, and she'd find a way to wrap up the Martin case.

And if she still couldn't convince Seth that things between them would work out? She'd think about that then.

CHAPTER TEN

"YOUR APARTMENT SHOULD be safe, but we wish you'd reconsider," Runnels stated once he and Stone had driven Seth and Charlie to her apartment.

Seth agreed with them, but Charlie wasn't having any of it. He watched as she walked through her small but cozy place, checking this and that, nodding as they told her where they'd searched, scanned and scavenged.

He felt a tug on his heartstrings as he saw her examining a large bouquet of flowers, a colorful mix of carnations and daisies, sitting on her small dinette table. Then she seemed to snap out of her reverie and remember why they were all there because her face hardened and she straightened her back and brushed her fingers through her hair like she was tense.

She didn't seem upset, only determined about something she wasn't discussing with any of them, even him. He figured maybe she'd open up once the others had left.

But as soon as Stone and Runnels left, with instructions that they should remain there unless accompanied by the man they had positioned outside her door, she went to the bathroom and shut the door.

Seth busied himself looking about, making mental notes and wondering if he'd been there before. Looked like a two-bedroom apartment, moderately-priced, nothing too fancy, certainly nothing ostentatious. A few personal items here and there, photographs and books, but nothing that required high maintenance, like plants or fish or pets. Typical cop pad, he thought, smiling grimly. She probably didn't spend much time here except to sleep between shifts.

Charlie left the bathroom and headed for her bedroom and closed the door. She had her cell phone pressed to her ear.

Seth stood outside it, talking to her. "Where are you going? I know you're leaving." He had no idea, but his intuition had kicked in, and he knew her well enough to realize she couldn't remain isolated. "Charlie, you heard what they said."

She cracked her door to talk to him but continued whatever it was she was doing. "What would you have me do? Sit in here like some victim, waiting for Rogers to make the next move? I don't operate like that."

Is she talking to me or whoever it is on the phone? Seth opened the door farther. She was sitting on the bed, changing from the loafers she'd worn into a pair of leather sneakers, lacing them furiously. She still had her cell phone against her ear, using a shoulder to buffer it, and she was talking in hushed tones, but he could make out part of her conversation.

"I'll explain later. Just do it, okay?"

Seth cleared his throat to get her attention without being too intrusive. He knew he shouldn't give a damn who she was talking to if she was planning to escape, but it needled him that she relied on someone else when he was right there. "Charlie, where are you going?"

She released the cell phone and continued lacing her shoes. "To the precinct."

"And how do you plan on sneaking past the guard outside?"

She looked up and set her jaw before replying. "You're going to distract him for me."

"Like hell!" Seth fumed. He burst through the door, giving only a cursory thought to her privacy. "Charlie, forget the Feds and their agenda. Think about your safety. What if Rogers is waiting for you?"

"Then he'll be staring at the door to my apartment and see me leave, which is fine by me. It'll take his focus off of you."

Seth blinked. She was protecting him? His blood boiled. "Sweet of you, dear," he said with a saccharin drip to his voice, "but I can take care of myself."

"I'm not trying to emasculate you, dear," she shot back. "I've seen what you can do when you're cornered, remember?" She lowered her head and appeared to be concentrating on a lace that wouldn't cooperate, muttering, "Freakin' contortionist."

He figured she was referring to the shoulder-popping incident at the love motel in Mexico. "You haven't seen anything yet."

Seemingly finished with dressing, Charlie planted both feet on the floor but remained seated on the edge of her bed. She eyed him warily, silent for a moment, her expression blank. Seth watched as her face softened.

Charlie nodded. "You're probably right." She stretched, flexing and rolling her head as if popping her neck. "My head hurts now, probably just a tension headache." She grinned ruefully. "Do me a favor?"

He placed his hands on his hips. "What?" he asked warily.

"Get me a glass of water so I can take an aspirin?" She patted her bed and cocked an eyebrow playfully. "Since we can't go anywhere, maybe we can both just lie down for a while. Of course, you'll need to take off that leather jacket if you want to be more comfortable." She raised her eyebrows, flirting with him.

He didn't trust her, but he couldn't find fault with her assessment of their situation, and even if all they did was lie there in one another's arms, it was better than sitting around worrying and waiting.

"Glasses are to the right of the sink," she instructed. "And the aspirin is in the medicine cabinet of the bathroom. Thanks."

Seth cocked an eyebrow. "You asking or nagging?"

"You decide." She grinned.

He watched as she slowly lay back on her bed. *Okay, Charlie, I'm game.* He pivoted and walked back to the bathroom. He quickly found the bottle of pills and shook two of them onto his palm. Then he went to the front of the apartment and into the kitchen.

While he busied himself looking for the glasses, he thought he heard a click, but when he remained still for a moment he heard nothing. Thinking he'd imagined the noise, he continued doing her bidding.

But when he walked back to her bedroom door, he found it shut. He rapped softly on the door. "Charlie?" He listened intently. Nothing. This time he knocked louder, repeating her name. Again, nothing.

Seth tried the doorknob. It was locked. What the hell? "If you wanted to be alone, all you had to do was tell me to—" He stopped speaking as realization washed over him. She'd played him. He knew without breaking down the door that Charlie was no longer in the apartment. She'd most likely gone out her bedroom window.

Given the choice of crashing through the door, and most likely getting her in trouble with the landlord, or accepting that she'd duped him, Seth popped the aspirin he'd brought for her into his mouth, swigged the water and went back into the living room. With any luck, his former coworkers would have someone waiting for her and would escort the little minx back to the front door.

SHE FELT BAD FOR involving her father and Julio in her deception, but Charlie didn't see much of a choice. Getting Sam to drive her to meet Julio was surprisingly easy because he was more curious than he was concerned for her safety—he knew she could take care of herself and whatever situation presented itself.

Julio, however, was a macho Latino whose code of honor forbade allowing a woman to jeopardize herself, even for the sake of justice.

"Are you out of your mind?" He plopped onto the barstool beside her at the pub where she'd told him to meet her. Julio rattled off a string of words in Spanish, with Charlie only catching every other syllable, most of them words she'd only heard when she was a beat cop in southwest Houston.

"You said you talked with the doctor in California, the one who was Seth's chief plastic surgeon," she persisted.

"Talk with him, querida? I spoke with him in person."

Charlie gasped. "He was here?"

"No no. I flew to Los Angeles." Julio held up his hands before she could protest. "My family has money, and I wanted to see my cousin in L.A. anyway, okay? So don't get bent out of shape, it was nothing out of pocket for me necessarily." He smiled engagingly. "My father was happy to help."

Charlie's mental calculator added up the expensive shoes, the hair, the dental work she'd suspected

Julio had done—nobody had teeth that perfect without help, not to mention the fancy motorcycle she'd seen him ride. It all made sense now, that he'd come from money prior to entering the academy. She suppressed a grin at his animated face while he explained his trip.

"First I went to his office—*Dios mío.* This man has money falling out of his..." Julio stopped himself. "Sorry. Anyway, *dinero de sobra,* lots of money." He went on to describe the building, the office, the staff. "I made nice with his receptionist and told her what I needed, information as to who paid for your friend's operations." A self-satisfied grin crossed his handsome features. "I took her to a really nice restaurant, a new one owned by that actor who was in..."

"And?" Charlie prompted impatiently.

"It wasn't the sister—it was that Rogers fellow, the guy who came into the office while you were in Guadalajara. Lots of nerve, wouldn't you say?" Julio's incredulity was displayed in every gesture, every word. "I mean, the man has the *cojones* to walk into a room full of cops and act like he's just a concerned citizen or employer, and the whole time he's up to his *cuello* in this thing?" Julio drew a finger across his neck to illustrate.

"He's probably the one who killed Martin," Charlie said. She explained what she'd heard from the Feds. "I'm supposed to be bait so that he'll talk to me or Seth, but I wouldn't put it past this guy to shoot first and ask questions later, you know?"

"I wouldn't let him near my sister, I can tell you that," Julio said, agreeing. "I told you he's dirty, didn't I? This man is probably responsible for God knows how many deaths of American citizens."

He went on to complain about the traitorous dereliction of duties on both sides of the Red River, and Charlie let him rant for a few moments while she collected her thoughts. It would be one thing to simply do as the CIA had requested and let Rogers approach her or Seth, but if Rogers was as deeply involved in terrorist trafficking, wouldn't it be better to follow him, to keep watch on his activities?

The Feds had most likely done just that, but somehow the slippery creep had eluded them, so what made them think he'd cooperate even if he was caught?

She shuddered at the thought of meeting up with Rogers without backup. He surely hadn't gotten by with his machinations as long as he had without being extremely careful.

"Let me go to the station and talk to Bemo," she suggested. "I'm sure he's feeling pretty bad if they've had him keep me out of the loop. Once I pick his brain, then retrieve a couple of items from my desk—"

Julio interrupted her. "Wouldn't it be better if I picked up whatever you needed and saved you the ass-chewin' you'll receive from the captain for dodging the Feds?"

"No, thanks. I'd rather get this over with," she said.

Julio held up his hands. "Okay, but I tried."

WHEN THERE WAS a knock at Charlie's door thirty minutes later, all Seth could think was *took you long enough.* But to his surprise, it wasn't Charlie being escorted by CIA. It was a tall, burly man who was a much heavier, more masculine version of his errant lover.

"What's a smart guy like you doing opening the door without first checking the Judas hole?" A big man of about sixty pushed the door wide and stared at Seth.

"Say what?" Seth blinked in surprise.

"The damned peephole. We call it a Judas hole. You must be Seth." The big man didn't wait for Seth to comment and didn't really wait for him to move—he just pushed his way into the apartment.

Seth took in the guy's attire—same type of laid-back clothing he saw on Charlie before she left. Leather sneakers, jeans, T-shirt and jacket, only this time with a University of Houston Cougars baseball cap completing the picture.

Giving Seth a long, drawn-out once-over, the man reached out his hand for Seth to shake. "Name's Sam."

Seth took the firm grip, wanting to wince and

laugh at the testosterone-inflated clench Charlie's father applied.

"Thought I'd come back and check out the man who seems to have captured my baby girl's attention. You don't mind, do you?" Sam asked.

"Not at all." Seth felt out of place motioning for Sam to sit down, considering it was Charlie's home, not his, so instead he took a seat and hoped Sam would follow suit. He did.

Then it struck Seth that, of course, it had to have been Sam who picked up Charlie and drove her to wherever she went. "You were the one who came after her when she snuck out?" he asked.

"She'd have done it anyway," Sam said. "Figured it might as well be me helping her, than leaving her with her butt hanging out of her bedroom window and being on foot once she dropped to the ground."

"Where…?"

"Some cop bar near her precinct," Sam responded. "She said something about talking to her new partner, then speaking to her captain. She's a little ticked off that he played ball with the Feds without telling her, but she understands. Said she did, anyway."

Seth didn't know who the more alpha male was, but he found himself doing the same thing as Charlie's father, sizing up the other man in the room and making mental comparisons, wondering if he could take him should the need arise, and hoping like hell that they'd find themselves on the same side of the fence should a dividing line be drawn. Sam seemed quite capable of standing alone, but he'd make a formidable ally, inspiring confidence in a comrade and kicking butt and taking names of their opponents.

"What say we take a drive?" Sam asked.

"Sure." Didn't matter where to at that point. Just the idea of freedom with a strong man at his back sounded good.

"First let me talk to the guy at the end of the hall, the one watching the apartment. He's not one of the fellows I met yesterday in here." Sam chuckled, as if at a private joke. "But they gave him my name because I told them I'd be back to see my daughter once she got home."

Sam rose. "Anyway, give me a couple of minutes, let him check with his superiors, and I'll come back for you once we get the go-ahead." He looked around. "You have a piece of paper or a cell phone?"

Seth nodded. "Phone's in the kitchen. Let me get it." Once he found the item, he plugged in the number Sam gave him.

Sam paused at the door after opening it. "I'll fill the tank with gas while our friend out there gets hold of his boss, and I'll give you a call in about ten or fifteen minutes."

BEMO, AS USUAL, was in his office earlier than scheduled, and he wasn't pleased to see Charlie. "Figured you'd show up," he said, motioning for her to have a seat across from him. He pulled out a folder and opened it, rifling through the papers inside until he found what he wanted. Then he turned the ensemble clockwise until it faced her.

He stabbed at a photo. "Damien Rogers. Only time I ever heard of that first name was when I watched those old movies about the devil."

Charlie nodded. "I know the ones." She read through his profile. "Looks like he may be the spawn of the devil after all, doesn't it?"

"He's pretty bad." Bemo pulled out a sheet for her to read. "At first, our boys from Washington thought he didn't know about your friend, the one whose photo was in your desk."

She was surprised. "Julio showed you?"

"He did." Bemo's face looked perplexed. "Did you know his father was Senator Rodríguez from Austin?"

She shook her head. "Not surprised, though, not after what he told me earlier." She relayed what Julio had mentioned about his family having money. Then she updated Bemo on Julio's discovery that Rogers paid for Seth's surgeries.

"Ah, so the bastard knew all along." Bemo thumped his desk with a fist. "That's all they need to tie him to the trafficking in Mexico. We've already established that Aldridge and his sister were involved, so there's the link."

Charlie watched, then listened as Bemo picked up his phone and dialed a number, leaving a message for Stone on his voice mail to call him ASAP.

"Thank God," she said with a note of satisfaction

once he'd left the message. "Maybe we won't have to get involved any further."

Bemo lifted a finger. Evidently, Stone had picked up on the other end. Charlie's hopes were dashed as she watched her captain's face.

"I'm not surprised," Bemo said, cutting Charlie a sour look.

What the hell did I do? Bemo hadn't seemed all that angry with her when she'd shown up at the precinct, so why was he pulling an attitude with her at this point?

She didn't have to wait long. Once he hung up, he placed both hands on his desk and leaned forward toward her. "What is your father doing picking Seth up at your apartment?"

Charlie shrugged. "I think he just wanted to buy him a beer, get to know him. Why?"

"Well, they should have stayed put. Seems our federal buddies can't reach their guard standing point at your apartment now, and it wasn't ten minutes ago that he got their permission to let Seth leave with your dad. Any idea where they'd have gone?"

The look on his face prompted her to ask "Why?"

"Because while Sam left his number with Stone, nobody is able to reach him now. Your father and Taggart seem to have vanished, as has their guard. Either that or… Just find them, okay?"

She stood, reaching for her shoulder bag. "I'll go home and see if they left a note. That doesn't make sense, though. Sam always answers his phone." *Unless something has happened to him.*

Fear shot through Charlie, electrifying her with terror. She tried calming herself. The Houston metropolis was a large area in which to get lost, but Sam was a creature of habit. There were only a small number of places where she figured he'd have gone.

"One other thing," Bemo said, halting her before she left. "Stone's in Washington, about to board a plane back to Houston, and he can't reach that other guy I met with him. Run-something."

"Runnels?"

"Yeah. You'd think with all of their fancy surveillance equipment and protocol that they could keep in touch with one another better. Anyway, if Runnels is there, tell him Stone says to stay put, whatever that means. Stone wants Runnels in the local branch office when he gets back, in other words."

"THAT WAS QUICK," Seth marveled when he heard the knock at the door. Sam hadn't been gone but ten minutes. There must be a convenience store or gas station close by.

As he reached for the doorknob he remembered what Sam had said about checking the Judas hole, but he knew it had to be Charlie's father. Who else would it be? Charlie had a key.

A split second later he wished like hell he'd done the smart thing. The door flung open, bumping him hard and destroying his equilibrium, and two men he didn't recognize were on him in a flash, beating him about the face and hitting him on the head, then whirling him around, forcing him to the ground.

Scattered memories collided with current actions, and Seth's mind raced to connect the dots to form a picture. Speech—shoes—hands—clothes. His head throbbed where he'd been hit, but he steeled himself to focus. They spoke Spanish. One wore ratty dark blue sneakers, and Seth was certain that was the man who'd punched him in the face and then whacked him on the head. Seth couldn't see his hands, but he was pretty sure he'd just been assaulted with the butt of a gun.

The other wore brown leather slip-ons. The man with brown shoes had a gold band encircling the forefinger of his left hand and a larger ring with a garnet on his ring finger—Seth didn't get a good look at his right hand.

Sneaker man wore jeans. Brown-and-gold man wore polyester pants. Both reeked of alcohol and cigarettes, and the one who reminded Seth of an eighties Las Vegas lounge singer needed a breath mint. Baaad.

Since they didn't speak to one another, only cursed at him in Spanish as they hoisted him to his feet and bound his hands in front of him, Seth was pretty sure that whatever they had planned for him had been well-orchestrated, that this wasn't some random mugging or robbery. And he'd bet every penny Aldridge had spent on his mansion that the guard who had been posted in the hall was dead.

Sadly, when the two men escorted him out of the apartment and toward the stairs, he saw that he was right. A quick glance at the guard's crumpled figure told Seth the guy had been shot multiple times, most likely with the gun that had been used to beat Seth.

Seth stole a glance at the denim-clad man and saw the silencer on the barrel of the nine millimeter.

The one thing that gave him hope was that Sam was nowhere in sight, so maybe he hadn't gotten caught in the crossfire.

"OH, NO!" CHARLIE DREW her gun as she saw the man lying face down mere yards from her apartment door. She immediately radioed for backup. She could see from her position that her door was open, and fear gripped her heart. She knew she should wait, but every cell in her body screamed to know what lay beyond that open door. Would she find her dad or Seth…or both of them…in a pool of blood?

"Dad!" she called. "Seth!"

The elderly woman in the apartment next to hers cracked open her door, and Charlie yelled at her to get back inside. Another nearby neighbor did the same thing, most likely out of curiosity as to why anyone would be bellowing, and Charlie advised him likewise to remain where he was.

Daddy, where are you? Her training to wait for backup warred with her natural instincts to protect those she loved. *Seth, please, please be all right.*

Tears of frustration stung her eyes, and she wiped them away angrily. She knew better than to get emotional—her life depended upon her ability to remain calm and in control.

Her cell phone rang, and she nearly cried with relief when the display showed one word—Sam.

"Dad! Where are you?"

Silence at the other end of the phone. Charlie's resolve not to panic collapsed. Why didn't he answer?

She looked at the display again—the phone was dead. Almost as quickly as it had died, the phone sprang to life with another call from Sam.

"Sorry," he said. "I hit the wrong button and cut us off."

Charlie sobbed with relief. "You're alive."

"Where are you, Charlene?" His voice was grave.

"I'm at the apartment."

"They killed that guard, didn't they?" Sam asked.

"How do you know? Daddy, where the hell are you? Where's Seth?"

Charlie heard the sirens as her backup arrived. "Dad, hang on. Is Seth inside?"

"No, baby. They took him. I got here in time to see two men walking him out to their car."

"What?" Charlie felt like she was operating an old PBX phone station, using both hands, arms, everything but her feet, to direct her fellow officers and manage the call with her father. She stopped talking to Sam long enough to explain what she knew of the situation to the cop running point.

As the others crept toward her apartment, Charlie

hung back to finish the call. "Say that again? What men?"

Sam told her the make, model, even the tag number of the vehicle the three men with Seth had.

Three men? Seth didn't stand a chance.

"Charlene, he was alive when they stuffed him into that car, and I haven't heard any gunshots, but you need to call your partner in case I lose them."

Charlie felt a mixture of hope and despair. So Seth and the three men were in a moving vehicle, not at their destination, and Sam was behind them.

"So where the hell have you been?" she asked.

"Buying a new charger for my cell phone." Sam sounded perturbed. "I know, I know. If I'd just gone back earlier, he might still be there."

Charlie thought a moment. "Or you'd both have been captured."

CHAPTER ELEVEN

SETH TICKED OFF DETAILS, hoping his faulty memory would recall them all, but what he noticed most about his predicament was that, as when he was with Charlie, his body remembered things his mind didn't. His first inclination was for fight then flight, but something told him to remain calm. If they were going to kill him, they'd have done it already. No, they were taking him to meet someone…his former employer, the man responsible for Martin's and Lawson's deaths.

He was stuffed into the backseat between the two men who had abducted him, his face pushed between his knees. They told him to remain quiet, and he did just the opposite. As soon as the driver gunned the engine, Seth reared his head and gouged both men in the ribs at the same time. *Not my fault you tied my hands in front of me.*

With his fists, he slammed each man in the face, first one—then the other, busting their noses. Then he leaned to the side, grasping Mr. Denim's gun hand and aiming it at Mr. Las Vegas before Vegas could fire off a round. With Vegas pulling a bead on him and Denim's fingers reflexively struggling to get off a shot of his own, the outcome was inevitable.

Denim shot Vegas, with Seth aiming the gun. One man down, two to go.

Seth quickly grabbed the gun when Vegas dropped it then shoved his body against the fallen man to be able to detect if the creep was still alive. Then Seth leveled the downed man's gun on the driver, and soon he, the driver and Denim were in a triangular stand-off, with Denim shakily holding a gun on Seth and Seth holding one on their driver.

"Shoot me, and we all die," Seth warned Denim.

"How about I just shoot you anyway, you crazy bastard?" Denim spurted blood as he spoke.

"Doesn't matter to me," Seth told him, "because you'll kill me anyway. I might as well take you two down with me."

The driver pitched forward as if grabbing something from underneath the seat, and Seth quickly shot through the car's seat cushion, causing the driver to scream in pain, swerve and clutch his butt.

"You want some of this?" Seth asked Denim as the startled man continued shaking, aiming and yelling.

Denim screamed obscenities and told their driver to keep driving.

"Doesn't matter to me," Seth repeated. All the while his eyes darted from Denim's eyes to his trigger finger, watching for the first flinch and preparing to kill. Whatever type of man he'd been before, he knew in that instant that he was trained to survive and that he detested killing anyone, so he prayed Denim would be smart. If it got bloody, then so be it, but Seth wasn't letting them kidnap him because he knew as sure as he was staring at them that they had every intention of killing him if there was anything left after Rogers got through with him.

"What's your name?" Seth asked the man in the backseat with him. "I can't go on thinking of you as the guy with bad taste in clothing."

"Fuck you." Denim swung the gun at Seth's face.

"I don't think so." Seth fired the gun directly into the man's gun hand then swiftly banged him on the temple with the butt of the gun he'd confiscated from his other kidnapper.

The car ground to a halt, and before the driver could reach for his door handle, Seth placed the gun in the back of his skull. "You've already got a constipation problem with bullets. Want to go for a headache as well?"

The man sat stock-still. "No." His voice quivered with pain and fear.

"Press the release on the trunk, then hand me the keys," Seth commanded, waiting while the driver did as told. "Now lie down across the front seat with your face pressed against the leather and your hands across the back of your head where I can see them."

Then Seth instructed Denim to get out and crawl into the trunk.

"But I'm bleeding, man!" Denim wailed.

“Guess you should have told me your name.” Seth heard a car door several feet away slam shut, and he hoped it was someone with a cell phone who could call the cops because he couldn’t afford to take his eyes off the two men he’d wounded.

“Shut up, Geraldo.” The man with his face buried in the front seat complained. “At least you can sit.”

“Geraldo, huh?” Seth pushed aside the first man he’d shot and unlatched the back door. He crawled out, gun still trained on Geraldo. “Nice and easy, Geraldo. At least with one hand you can fight those who want to make you their girlfriend in prison.”

“Fuck that.” Geraldo stared cold black daggers at Seth. “I ain’t goin’ back there.”

Seth lifted his eyes to see strong hands grasping Geraldo by the waist and hauling him out of the car backward.

“Thank Christ!” Geraldo babbled. “This crazy mother—”

Sam’s ironic laughter was like a symphony to Seth’s ears. “Oh, don’t you wish you had someone else coming to your rescue?” He boxed Geraldo’s ears and slammed his body against the car. “Spread ’em, and consider your rights having been read to you as if I was still on the force.”

Seth met Sam’s gaze across the hood of the car, and Sam nodded.

“Of course, my buddy over there,” Sam told Geraldo. “I believe he can still recite the words you love to hear.”

Seth nodded and proceeded to deliver the Miranda to both Geraldo and his friend with the bullet in his butt. He'd no sooner finished than he heard the first plunk, then the next…and he saw Sam fall to the ground.

When he whirled to see who had fired the shots, he stared in disbelief as Runnels held a gun in his face. The bastard shrugged without smiling. Then as Seth stared in horror, he watched as the Fed finished off the driver and Geraldo. Finally he spoke.

"Sorry, Seth."

CHARLIE ARRIVED AT the location Sam had given her, and her blood froze.

"Oh, no, Daddy! No!" She raced to where he lay and felt his pulse. It was thready, but it was there. She kissed his face, then ripped open his shirt, feeling the hard Kevlar beneath her fingers.

As it dawned on her he'd worn his old vest, she was giddy with relief. "Oh, God, Sam. You kept not only your gun but your vest."

He stirred in her arms, swearing as he came around. "Oh, shit, that hurts." He tried to sit up, struggling against the constraints of the vest, wincing.

Charlie heard footsteps and turned to see Julio coming up behind her.

"*Hijo de puta!*" Julio knelt beside Charlie and Sam. "I radioed for backup and an ambulance. Thank God he's alive."

"Yeah, but that bastard took Seth," Sam complained. "One of those guys I clobbered at your house, Charlene."

"What? Who?"

"Think his name starts with an R."

Charlie stood and with Julio's help got Sam to his feet. "What men? The Feds?"

"Yeah, the tallest one with the buzz cut."

"Runnels?"

"That's the one. Big guy. I saw him coming up but never put two and two together until after it was too late."

She wanted to cry. The whole time she and Seth were with Runnels and Stone, one of them was feeding Rogers information.

"What about his partner?" Julio asked. "If one's dirty—maybe the other?"

"One way to find out," Charlie said. "Call Bemo and tell him what's happened."

Julio did as she suggested while Charlie tended to her father. "What were you thinking?" She helped rid him of the bulletproof vest.

"I thought we'd have coffee, that I'd get him out of your apartment, get to know him." Sam's voice was gruff, and he moaned a couple of times as Charlie felt his ribcage. "Leave me alone—I'm fine, just sore."

"You need to get checked out."

"What I need is my gun and a helicopter so I can follow them. Don't suppose you'd have one of those handy, would you?"

Charlie started to respond but paused, thinking. She looked up at the street light and saw the camera attached. "No, but I have the next best thing." She quickly dialed Bemo's cell number. "Did Julio give you our location? How about pulling feed from the camera at this intersection and checking for a license plate and the direction that car went afterward?"

Sam leaned against the abandoned vehicle when she was done. "How soon before we can leave this intersection?"

Charlie looked around. "Maybe fifteen or twenty minutes? They'll need to take your statement."

"You take it."

"Member of the family, Dad. Someone else needs to take both our statements." She motioned for Julio to come back over.

Sam rubbed his sore chest and stomach. "Damn, but that still hurts. Beats taking the bullet, though."

She guffawed, choking back a sob. "You're like a cat in clover. You miss this."

"Like hell." He gave her a lopsided grin. "Maybe just a bit. Don't miss it enough to give up my retirement."

Charlie leaned against the car next to him. Professionalism warred with personal feelings of inadequacy in not knowing yet how to help Seth. "He's screwed, isn't he?"

Her father sighed. "Depends upon whether or not he catches a break, a moment when nobody's paying enough attention. He doesn't seem like a talkative sort, not like your new partner, so I suspect he'll have to rely on intuition instead of baffling them with bullshit."

She blinked back the tears. "No, he's not much of a conversationalist, but he's smart. He'll figure out a way to outmaneuver them."

Charlie's heart broke. She'd lost him once—she couldn't conceive of losing him again, this time permanently.

Her life had been full before she'd met him, but it hadn't been complete. She'd rediscovered a relationship with a father who'd been absent during most of her formative years. She'd come to peace with a mother who was a few sandwiches shy of a picnic. Her career was everything she could have hoped for...and more. Maybe she didn't have the exceptional paychecks or exciting nightlife many of her friends did, but she'd been happy. The thought of a future without Seth, however, was unimaginably bleak, and the thought of not having him near, not being able to talk to him, to feel his touch...it was devastating.

"I can't lose him again, Dad. He has to stay alive until we can reach him."

Sam reached for her hand. "I hope he will, baby girl."

Seth knew better than to struggle against the odds he faced. Better to do as Runnels said and go along peacefully. He knew without a doubt, though, that Runnels would kill him in an instant and that his plans were to do just that anyway, once he and Rogers had whatever information they needed.

He thought fast. The only thing keeping him alive was the fact that Runnels and Rogers had no idea just how much Seth had recalled after that meeting with Stone and Runnels or if Seth had divulged what he'd remembered to a third party. He had—Charlie. Charlie knew as much as he did, which meant that if he couldn't escape and reach her before they did, she'd be dead.

Seeing Sam get shot had been a nightmare. The only thing that puzzled Seth, in retrospect, was the stance Runnels had used—definitely not anything he'd learned at the academy, more like a street fighter who held the gun sideways like some big city thug gangsta wannabe.

Seth's initial reaction had been panic until he remembered what a bullet hitting bone or muscle sounded like, and what he'd heard was similar but not exact. The old man had evidently kept most of his gear when he retired. So most likely Sam was alive unless someone else had followed behind Runnels to complete the job.

Doubtful. Runnels wasn't the type who needed someone to clean up after him, and he wasn't afraid of doing the dirty work himself, if the executions Seth had witnessed were indicative. Geraldo and his accomplices had been wounded and therefore a hindrance to Runnels, so they had to be silenced before anyone found them, and blood left a pretty well-telegraphed trail. No medical facility would have touched them without filing a report, and the men wouldn't have survived long without attention. Seth felt guilty for having shot both of them, even though he hadn't aimed to kill, merely to keep from being murdered.

Now it looked as if he was worse off than he'd been with the three bumbling kidnappers.

Seth sat in stony silence beside Runnels, mindful of the Uzi Runnels held. They were the only ones in the backseat of the car, and Seth didn't recognize the driver. Somehow he didn't feel so betrayed because he didn't believe Stone was in on this mess, but Seth wondered where the guy was. Had Runnels killed him?

The driver was young, probably only in his early twenties. Just a kid, Seth thought ruefully, and one with a short life ahead of him if he was already hooked up with the likes of Rogers and Runnels. He seemed extremely nervous as he steered their car through traffic. His eyes kept darting to Seth's, and there was something frightened yet sympathetic in his gaze.

Seth noted with a sinking feeling that this time he wasn't told to ride with his head between his knees, meaning Runnels wasn't concerned with keeping him in the dark about wherever they were headed. It wasn't important for Runnels and Rogers to protect their privacy if they intended to kill him.

"IF I'D WANTED TO WORK in dark, smelly places, I'd have joined the city's sanitation department." The driver, who'd parked the car inside the dank, warehouse-like garage, looked about nervously once they'd arrived at their destination.

"Shut up, Kevin." Runnels gave the kid a hard stare. "You get paid well to drive fast and think slow." He opened his door, cautioning Seth. "Out, this way, slowly."

Seth did as told, taking in the empty building. If Rogers was there, he blended into the walls.

"You realize you'll never be able to run for office once you're back in D.C., right?" He hoped his smart mouth wouldn't write checks his bound hands and shackled memory couldn't cash, but he needed to stall, give himself time to look around his new location.

Runnels, who had barely cracked a smile since Seth had arrived from Mexico, suddenly burst into laughter. When he did, Seth noticed the bad teeth. Then Runnels tossed his head as he laughed, and Seth noticed the tattoo. Whatever he was, Runnels was not CIA.

"I take it you killed our real agent?" The words were bitter in Seth's mouth as he realized yet another of his comrades had been murdered.

Runnels' jaw dropped slightly. He seemed to know his tattoo had given him away, for he touched it gingerly. "Well, well, you must be regaining some of your lost senses, Agent Taggart." Runnels snorted.

"Pity that the man who really graduated the academy with you wasn't as bright."

Seth narrowed his eyes. The voice, the crooked smile, the Midwestern accent. The wreck in Mexico and the figure of a tall man in jungle fatigues hovering over him. Runnels, of course—well, someone posing as Runnels. That explained the reaction he'd felt when he and Charlie had first met the man. *He was the one standing over me in the rain in Guadalajara.*

"What are you?" he asked the man. "Some mercenary?"

"Please. The term is derogatory. We prefer to call ourselves contractors." He smirked. "Or guns for hire, if you choose."

Seth swallowed a retort. So the man saw himself as a cowboy of sorts. Let him. Even they met the long arm of the law at times. Maybe this arrogant fool would as well.

While the three of them waited in the garage, or whatever it was, Kevin paced nervously, to the point that the gunman barked at him to get back in the car if he couldn't be still. And Kevin obliged, reclaiming his place behind the wheel. One look at the boy's face told Seth that Kevin had wanted to be back there for some reason. *Probably because he knows what they're about to do to me.*

Not long afterward, a door creaked, and Seth heard footsteps, and with each footfall he knew his time was limited. He wondered what Rogers would do before killing him—and he was sure by this time that Rogers was the only one left who wanted to deal with him.

As soon as the man stepped into view, Seth recognized him. Within a millisecond, the key to unlock what had been hidden from him appeared, and that one face unleashed a flood of memories…and emotions.

Rage at what he'd witnessed.

Damien Rogers, the smarmy businessman with minions who worked behind the scenes at Simple Solutions, employing unsuspecting immigrants who thought they were merely helping bring their own families across the border, when once they'd been compromised and promised paradise, had been forced to spirit terrorists from other countries into America, along with their parents and children. If the employees who posed as companions, dates or surrogates of some sort for their contacts balked? Rogers would either pass the opportunity to see a loved one on to someone more willing to do his bidding—or worse, he'd threaten them with exposure and deportation.

Marjorie Lawson had been one such client. She had asked for someone to pose as her date for an important business meeting in Guadalajara, someone who spoke Spanish and was willing to travel. Her CIA cover had been that of an entrepreneur who exported leather goods. She'd been working undercover for two years and had already infiltrated

Rogers' organization, so the CIA had felt comfortable in sending her back for one more mission, this time with George Martin. Only something had gone terribly wrong, and Martin had disappeared. That's when Rogers had replaced him with Seth.

It all made sense now. Martin must've cracked. Seth knew after meeting Charlie and seeing the crime photos at the station that Martin had been tortured.

Looks like I'm next. Seth braced himself, trying not to fall into an abyss of despair when Rogers brought out the Bowie knife, the one Seth figured had most likely gutted Martin.

"FOR GOD'S SAKE, CHARLENE!" Sam bellowed from the backseat, where he clung to what he called the "oh shit bar" to steady himself. "Slow down!"

"Want me to drive?"

The meekness of Julio's offer was laced with concern, which only ticked Charlie off further. "No, thanks." She glanced into her rearview mirror. "Hang on, Dad. I've been driving since I was fourteen."

"Too bad your mother didn't instruct you better." Sam's gruff response was growled, but at least he didn't yell this time.

Charlie tapped the navigation system. "If you want to help, Rodríguez, just watch for upcoming streets and tell me if there are any traffic delays."

"We didn't have those things when I was on the force," said Sam, whose voice seemed calmer.

Charlie knew her partner and father were only trying to help, to keep her from screaming and pulling out her hair, and while she appreciated their input, she'd rather they both remained silent. It'd only been a few minutes since they'd received the information she needed—the whereabouts of the car that had been seen when Seth had disappeared. With that message had been news that Agent Runnels was an imposter. The real agent's body had been discovered inside an offshore oil drum the week before, and the medical examiner had just identified the remains. The body was missing both hands and eyes.

With Stone directing CIA personnel from his plane, and the Houston PD able to use the more sophisticated surveillance equipment of the Feds, the two groups had managed to pinpoint the exact location of the car, and the building where they hoped Seth was being held.

The Houston PD liaison with the CIA broke into the mike Julio held. "Heat sensors from the helicopter show six people in the building. The SWAT task force is in position and closing, awaiting instructions. Another chopper is at the airport waiting for Agent Stone."

Julio looked at Charlie after acknowledging the dispatcher. "You get that?"

"Yep. We're about four minutes from destination."

Julio peered at the GPS on the dash. "Traffic jam of some sort two blocks ahead."

Charlie quickly veered to the left then peeled down a one-way, avoiding oncoming traffic and eliciting more cursing from Sam. "Sam, you stay in the car when we get there."

"Like hell!"

"Daddy, please. I need someone there in case this guy who has been impersonating Runnels has more men in the parking lot we don't know about."

Sam had to realize she was protecting him, and knowing him, he considered it babysitting, when he was fully capable of handling himself and providing backup. She didn't dare glance at him, though, because the tears she'd been holding back would gush forth, and the last thing she needed was to drop the ball for Julio. His life and hers depended upon her being able to conduct herself as she'd been trained.

Nothing she'd done up to this point, however, had held such personal stakes for Charlie. Her very life, that of her partner, her father and the man she loved were on the line, and even with luck, the odds that they'd all walk away today were slim to none.

The dispatcher's voice was replaced with that of Bemo, chastising Charlie for her trip down the one-way. He asked what the hell she thought she was doing, and Julio responded something about a shortcut to the parking lot. Charlie was too busy avoiding mishap to catch everything verbatim, but in the back of her brain she knew she would hear about it once this was over.

If she survived.

She tore through the remainder of oncoming traffic, whipped onto another side street, and pulled into the garage's parking lot, with Julio getting instructions on which entrance they should use.

The list of necessities was short. Firepower, vest and a final appeal to the Almighty.

CHAPTER TWELVE

"You are a hard man to kill, Agent Taggart," Rogers said, walking slowly toward Seth. "I know because I've tried several times."

Seth remained silent. He wouldn't give Rogers the satisfaction of a response, not fear, not even contempt.

The door they'd entered was closed, with small shards of light filtering through broken boards where outside damage had occurred, making the monster appear somewhat dark, as if standing with a spotlight behind him. But Seth could well imagine the features, soft from too much cholesterol, hard with hate.

Seth had despised him on sight, primarily for what he stood for, but also because of the sexist attitudes Rogers displayed toward women. While Seth had only been hired to "date" locally the first few months he'd been at Rogers's escort service in Houston, he'd been allowed that last trip to Mexico, most likely because Martin had given him up. But Seth couldn't condemn Martin. The poor man had probably been demented by the time he'd collapsed. Seth promised himself that no matter what Rogers did, he'd not give him what he wanted. He'd not compromise another agent. Or Charlie.

Slight movement to the rear of the garage alerted Seth that at least two more of Rogers's henchmen were there, ready to kill him upon command if he survived what Rogers had in store for him.

"I see the wheels clicking in your mind," Rogers said smoothly. "You know what's coming, so you might as well save us both the trouble." He shifted his attention to the mercenary. "Frank, what about the other three?"

Ah, another name, not that it'll do me much good. Seth watched as the man who had posed as Runnels stepped forward.

"Dead. I didn't have time for cleanup."

"So the car is still there?" Rogers grew angry.

"Sue me. Couldn't be helped. You said you were leaving Houston anyway, that it was too dangerous." Frank shifted his Uzi.

Probably more as a threat in case Rogers reproached him, thought Seth.

Before he could form another thought, Seth heard the sole car in the garage, its engine coming to life.

"What the hell?" Rogers looked over his shoulder and walked toward the car, his hands waving at Frank. "Get that little bastard."

The kid who had driven them had triggered the garage door opener, and glaring sunlight broke into the garage as the door lifted, but instead of backing up, as Seth had imagined the kid would do, he threw the car into gear and sped toward them.

Within seconds, two thoughts raced through Seth's mind. Either the kid was nuts, or he was on Seth's side. In either case, it didn't look good. Seth was sitting smack in the middle of the garage and would be hit as surely as would one, if not both, of the other men.

Frank aimed, fired and kept firing, advancing on the car as if he hadn't a care in the world other than to kill the kid. Rogers, on the other hand, dodged, moving sideways at first, then toward Seth, with nothing it seemed but the knife to arm him. The two men standing in the shadows protecting Rogers also let loose with a hail of bullets. Seth's heart nearly stopped as he recognized the sound of AK47s. Frank's Uzi might do some damage up close, but it was primarily for spraying and show from a distance. The assault rifles, on the other hand, were serious firepower aimed at the kid.

Kevin, however, didn't seem to care that he was being fired upon. He ducked, dodged and wove his way from the opening of the garage to the heart of the building. Then Seth watched in horror as the kid aimed the car straight for Rogers and gunned the engine, diving below the wheel, seemingly not caring that he'd hit both Rogers and Seth at that speed.

Seth heard the bump as Rogers's body bounced off the car, and he braced himself for the impact that was inevitable, just as he heard more gunshots and shouting from the garage door. He caught the word *police* and heard someone shout *FBI* before he felt himself propelled backward. The chair broke, and Seth's bad shoulder slammed into concrete. He rolled, trying to avoid having his head smashed like a melon against the garage floor.

When he groggily looked up, he saw the wheels of the car coming for him. Then the screeching sound of brakes being applied, a car door being opened and Kevin screaming obscenities at Rogers, saying something about "my mother."

"She had a son!" the kid screamed. "Marjorie Lawson had a family, you piece of shit! She had a husband, and three kids!" Kevin continued delivering kicks to Rogers, in the groin, the gut, the head.

Seth tried hanging on to his sanity. The car had stopped. He wasn't dead. Kevin would surely be six feet under soon if Frank had his way. Bullets were still flying, and others were in the garage taking down the two men whose forms he'd only seen, but Seth had no idea if his rescuers would reach Kevin in time.

He jerked against the rope, the broken chair. He screamed in pain as he felt his shoulder snap out of place, and he saw feet menacingly striding toward him.

One more time, please, one more time. With a violent wrenching, he tore himself loose from the chair and rolled, struggling with the rope and the dislocated shoulder. There was nothing to brace himself against, and he figured he probably wouldn't be able to stand anyway, so he took the only avenue of escape he saw—he rolled beneath the front end of the car and jammed his shoulder back into place.

To his right, also on the ground, he saw Rogers, still alive but moaning in pain, the knife, which had probably flown out of Rogers's hand when he was hit, lying beneath the left front wheel of the car, and he saw Kevin's feet. The kid was kicking the hell out of the downed man, cursing and blaming him for his mother's death.

Seth struggled, crawled toward the knife, and his fingers had barely closed over it when he felt the bullet hit his leg. Seth yelled, and with superhuman strength born of adrenaline and self-preservation, he freed the knife and turned on his side, facing the feet. He stabbed the foot closest to him and clung with both hands around the blade's handle as Frank jerked his foot back with a thundering scream.

Dragged somewhat from beneath the car, Seth scrambled to swing his legs out and wrap them around Frank's foot, then the attached leg, all the while doubled over and clinging for dear life to the knife until he felt another bullet graze his side.

With a victorious yell, Seth maneuvered one of his legs between both of Frank's and felled him like a giant oak. Both men on the ground at last, evening the playing field, he twisted and turned until he had the mercenary's head between his legs and finally had him facing the other direction.

Frank still had the gun, but Seth had his opponent's airway, trapped between two muscled thighs, and he squeezed with every ounce of strength he possessed. Still clutching the rope that had bound him, Seth let Frank out of the leg-lock long enough to get the rope around Frank's neck and his legs around Frank's waist.

With the bigger man on top of him, Seth turned into a human python, squeezing the life out of Frank. The Uzi went off again and again, but it was in the air, not trained on any particular target, and that's all Seth cared about.

"Not this time," he grunted, holding his grip on his would-be assassin.

Excruciating cold crept over Seth, and he realized he was losing consciousness. With one last breath, he tightened the rope…his legs…and he grasped the gasping man around the neck, placing one hand on the side of his face, the other on his chin. Seth gave a last ferocious wrench, heard the bones break and sighed just as he lost the strength to go on.

GUNFIRE CRACKLED all around her, and Charlie screamed as she saw her partner fall to the ground, clutching his shoulder, with blood spurting from somewhere near his temple. "Rodríguez is hit!" She inched toward him, willing him to live.

Julio let loose with a stream of swearing in Spanish, but he still clutched his gun and aimed it…so close to Charlie's face she thought he'd shoot her. She ducked, more out of instinct than knowing what Julio was up to, and she heard the grunt as Julio's bullet found its target.

The thug behind her fell within a hair's width of her back, and Charlie lunged toward Julio. "You might warn a girl next time." She touched his face and said a quick prayer—the head wound was superficial. Then she ripped open his shirt, her hands searching for the strap on his vest. The bullet he'd taken had missed the Kevlar and had lodged a millimeter out of the protected range, hitting his upper arm. So why was he holding his chest?

She pushed aside Julio's hands and looked at the vest. If it'd been a car that had received hail damage, it'd have been totaled. There were dents all over it, and it looked as if two bullets had pierced the vest.

"Damn, that hurts!" Julio's eyes were wild as he spoke, and the blood from his head wound kept gushing.

Charlie feared he'd pass out from blood loss. She cradled his head against her chest and screamed for help once more.

She peered through the residue of gunpowder and dust that had been kicked up during the raid, searching for Seth. She'd watched, horrified, as the car had sped toward him, and she'd seen Runnels go gunning for him and the boy, but she hadn't seen who was wounded—she'd only heard the shots and flinched, wondering who'd been the victim.

"Seth!" She called his name several times, listening for a response, but he didn't respond. "Seth, can you hear me?"

A member of the SWAT team approached. "The guy you looking for a tall guy wearing a light leather jacket and jeans?"

She didn't know. Charlie blinked back tears and shook her head. Then she remembered. "Yes! Is he alright?"

The man's face was grim. "He's been shot."

"What?" Charlie started to rise and almost dropped Julio's head onto the cement floor.

The SWAT cop nodded. "If it makes you feel any better, looks like he killed the guy who was going for him—broke his neck."

Julio grumbled. "I'll live—go to him."

Charlie wanted desperately to do just that, but the bleeding man in her arms was her partner. "Who is with him?" she asked the officer.

"One of the other guys. They've called for an ambulance—should be here any minute." He looked at Julio. "Looks like there'll be two passengers unless there's an extra bus."

Julio tried to sit up, only to have Charlie scold him soundly. "Get up and die, Julio." Then she looked around, remembering. "Sam? Dad? You here?"

Her father's voice hollered back.

"I knew it." The tears she'd held back began to

fall. "Old fart never listens to me. I told him to stay in the damned car."

Julio chuckled then coughed, and blood came from his mouth. He wiped his lips with the back of a hand. "Sounds like someone else I know."

"Charlene?" Sam sounded winded, like he'd been running. He holstered his .45 and knelt beside her. "Thank God you're okay."

"Seth's been shot." She choked on the words. Charlie pointed in the direction of the car. "I can't see what's happening from here."

"I'll have a look." Sam patted her shoulder and frowned at Julio. "That had to hurt."

Julio offered a weak smile. "Wore my vest, did everything right and still got shot. Go figure."

"You'd have had to wear a Kevlar body condom to avoid getting hit in this mess," Sam said. "Be right back."

She knew only seconds had ticked by, but it seemed like an eternity before she heard the wail of sirens. By the sound of it, there were at least two more cop cars and two ambulances.

She remained with Julio until the paramedics knelt beside her, taking his vitals and asking her questions. As if by rote, she rattled off what she knew had happened, what she'd seen when giving him a quick examination—just the two bullet wounds, one that seemed minor, the other much more serious.

Then she flew across the garage to the vehicle where two other medics and Sam tended to Seth.

Her father held out a hand. "Before you climb into that van alongside him, hand 'em over. If I know you, you're not leaving his side."

Charlie handed him her keys, peering behind him to watch as the paramedics raced to usher Seth into the vehicle. "I gotta go. What about your truck?"

Sam motioned toward a television camera crew that had shown up. "I know one of the reporters. I'll get him to drive your car back to your place."

She nodded. "See you at the hospital?"

"Yep." He kissed his daughter's cheek. "He's still breathing, you know. He's unconscious, but his color's not bad, so hang in there, baby girl. Try not to fret."

Charlie felt more fragile than ever and gave him a ferocious hug, whispering. "Thanks, Sam."

Sam's chest heaved with a deep breath beneath her embrace. "So you're not too mad at your old man for busting in like that?"

She shook her head. "I knew you couldn't stay out of a gunfight. Never have, never will." She punched him on the shoulders with her fists. "Even if it means risking your life and worrying your daughter into an early grave."

Sam held her away from him and bent to kiss her again, this time on the forehead. "And knowing you were in that garage—what do you think that was doing to me?"

The sobs she'd held back burst forth. "Damn it, Daddy. Why do we do this? Why this job, why us, why Seth?"

"Because somebody has to do it, and we're participants, not observers, Charlie." He chucked her under the chin. "Quit crying, or they'll think you're the one who's been shot instead of your partner."

She turned to see the medics wheeling Julio toward them on a gurney. One female EMT had a bag of fluids on an IV pole hooked up to him, and she was biting her lips.

When Charlie looked, she saw Julio flashing his pearly white teeth, flirting with the poor girl.

"That boy would have one foot in the grave and still make a pass at a pretty girl," Sam commented.

"Let's roll!" One of the EMTs tapped Charlie on the shoulder.

She released her father, climbed into the ambulance, and the door slammed behind her. As they sped toward the hospital, she took one last look at her father and waved, then focused her attention upon Seth.

Out of the corner of one eye, she saw a movement. Julio was trying to get her attention. She reached across the small space dividing them and squeezed the proffered hand.

His expression had changed from one of flirtation to pain, yet through his own discomfort, he was trying to reassure her. Charlie's heart melted. She didn't care if her partner saw her this vulnerable or not. She was worried about Seth, but extremely thankful Julio had been with her during the worst day of her career.

"How is he?" she asked the attending EMT.

The woman smiled. "If he's well enough to make eyes at me like he's been doing, he'll pull through just fine and have a couple of battle scars to impress the girls."

Charlie glanced back at Seth. She'd dared not look at him too intently before then, primarily because she didn't want to fall apart. Now, however, she couldn't have looked away. His pallor had changed, even during the past few minutes. He looked gaunt, and his lips had changed from pale pink to gray.

She glanced sharply at the machine monitoring him. His blood pressure was falling, and the machine started beeping.

The other EMT in the back of the van asked her to move away while he ripped open Seth's shirt and reached for the defibrillator, all the while talking to the other attendant and speaking to Seth in quiet, even tones. "We've got a bleeder! Stay with me, man."

Charlie gasped. The EMT's next few words swam in her brain. Transfusion. Tremendous loss of blood. Seth was going into cardiac arrest—he could die right there in front of her, and she was unable to help him.

Her heart thundered in her chest, and she flinched with every movement the medic made. She closed her eyes momentarily, unable to watch. She could barely breathe. The man she loved was dying? How could this be?

The next few seconds were a never-ending nightmare, fraught with fear, laced with dread and intensified by the montage of scenes unfolding before her. Seth—smiling at her over dinner that first night. Seth—making love to her, holding her, reassuring her that he'd be back soon from Mexico. Then Seth as Mason, Mason as Seth, the two images blurring and smearing her soul's canvas, coloring her world with shades of the unknown. Finally, just Seth, her lover, her friend, the one man to whom she could tell anything.

The piercing sounds of the machine as his heart stopped completely. Another sound, that of someone screaming—her. She opened her eyes and flew forward, shoving aside the shocked EMT, pounding Seth's chest.

"No!" she raged, her hands flying everywhere, thumping his chest, slapping his face. "Seth, don't you die on me, damn it! You do not have that right—you come back to me. Do you hear? Seth!"

Both EMTs grabbed her, one from behind, the other in front, and they ordered her aside, pushing her practically onto Julio's lap to get her away from the listless man on the opposite gurney.

Suddenly a new sound, that of beeping, a weak but sure sign of life coming from the dying man she'd just whacked.

"What?" The male EMT leaned closer toward Seth, and he shushed everyone else in the van. "What did you say, sir?"

Charlie listened, breath caught in her throat. One word—repeated—she listened, disbelieving, then burst into giggles as Seth said it again, his voice barely a fractured whisper.

"Nag, nag, nag."

CHAPTER THIRTEEN

"ONE BULLET TAGGED the fleshy party of his upper arm, another grazed his temple. He took two to the chest, and one pierced his lung, but we have him patched up." The male nurse pointed a thumb over his shoulder toward Julio's room. "He's not going anywhere for a few days."

Sam came to stand behind his daughter. "And Seth?"

One of the doctors entered their circle. "Are you the Vargases?" Once Charlie and Sam nodded, he continued. "Mr. Taggart signed the consent forms to discuss this with you and give you power of attorney. We have him scheduled for a series of MRIs. He has multiple abrasions and lacerations to his head, hands and hips, and a dislocated shoulder that has seen better days. We removed the bullet from his leg that nicked his femoral artery." He frowned. "You know about the shunts, right?"

Charlie and Sam shook their heads.

"He's agreed once he's stable to let us relieve some of the pressure from his brain by inserting shunts." The surgeon explained how they'd run tubes from Seth's skull down to his stomach, where the fluid would be emptied. "Of course, they'll have to be cleaned now and then, but he shouldn't need replacements for a couple of years or more."

When Charlie sobbed, the doctor patted her shoulder. "Your fiancé should be fine in a few weeks."

"Oh, he's not—we're not—engaged." Charlie recovered her shock at being mistaken for Seth's bride-to-be long enough to respond.

The doctor looked perplexed. "He's asking for you, you know?"

Charlie shook her head.

"Once the nurse leaves his room, you may go in," the doctor told her. "Just don't get him overly excited. He's had a rough day." He nodded curtly as he left to talk to another nurse at the center desk.

"Why do doctors always talk in understatements?" Sam complained. "Rough day? Not like he woke up, stubbed his toe and got a headache."

Charlie pointed toward Seth's glass-walled room, where she could clearly see Stone talking to Seth and the nurse writing something on a clipboard. "Why does he get to go in there, but I'm told to wait?"

"Maybe something to do with insurance?" Sam shrugged. "Does it matter? The man's alive. That's more than I can say for the guy whose neck he broke." Sam chuckled. "Damn, I'd like to have seen that fight."

"Daddy!"

Sam's eyes widened. "Sorry, kid. Forgot I wasn't

talking to just any cop but the one that's in love with him."

Charlie waited impatiently for Stone to leave Seth's room so she could visit. She glanced at her opaque reflection in the glass. She looked like she'd been through a war, clothes disheveled, face blotchy from crying, her hair standing out at all angles. Had she ever looked worse? She doubted it.

And Seth—dear, sweet man. He was as handsome as ever, even if he did have tubes running into him from all directions and that little plastic thingie in his nose so he could get oxygen.

Stone stepped aside, and Charlie saw Seth smile, and her throat ached from a lump she couldn't manage to swallow, shutting off her air for a moment. She finally sobbed, the lump dissolved and she was able to breathe. Weakly, she pressed her face against the glass and looked through it longingly.

Soon the two men saw her. She stepped away from the glass and dabbed her eyes as a fresh onslaught of tears threatened to burst.

Stone motioned for her to come in, and to her surprise the man hugged her briefly. He didn't say anything, but the look in his eyes made her wonder at what the two men had been discussing. Stone looked like he knew something she didn't.

"Hey, you." Seth's voice wasn't strong, but it was steady, almost cheerful. "I've missed you."

Charlie walked tentatively toward the bed, his expression coaxing her forward until she was at his side. She took his hand in hers then bent and held it to her cheek. The damned tears she'd struggled to keep from him flowed freely.

Seth's hand moved against her skin, and he stroked her face, wiping away the drops as they fell against his fingers. "Care to sit with me for a while?" he whispered.

Charlie dropped into the chair beside the bed, unable to speak. She was overcome with relief that he was alive. She didn't care what he said as long as she could hear his voice, reassuring her that he was still with her.

"I still have a job," Seth said, struggling for air, measuring his words carefully. "Washington office told Bill—Stone—that I can have one of the desk jobs in the Houston office if I want it." He paused before continuing. "What do you think?"

Charlie blinked, sniffed, found a tissue and blew her nose. "Whatever you want. You don't need my permission."

Seth cleared his throat. "Sorry. Hard to talk." He smiled ruefully. "Don't need you to validate my decision, but it'd be nice if...the woman I loved...was okay with it."

She took a deep breath. *The woman he loves?* "Seth." His name was a whisper on her lips.

"I love you, Charlie." This time his voice was ragged with emotion.

Charlie grabbed both his hands and squeezed. "I

love you, too. I don't care if you can't remember us—you know? The past."

"Ah. But I can." He returned the pressure she exerted on his hands. "Not everything, but most of it, I think, and I have you to help clear up what is fuzzy. It's funny, but what's there is at least solid. It's a foundation for something, don't you think?"

She wasn't sure what he meant, but she nodded. "Sure."

He chuckled. "You don't have a clue what I mean, do you?"

Charlie shook her head slowly. Now wasn't the time to play games with him. If she'd learned anything the past few days, it was that total honesty with him was more important than pretending.

"Maybe we'd better get your father in here," he suggested.

"You want to speak to Sam?"

"Well, in a minute. He's an old-fashioned guy. He might like it if I did this right and asked for his blessing."

Charlie was dumbfounded. "What?"

"I can't go on like this," Seth explained. "Life is too short as it is, and I don't want to spend another day without you in it, by my side. I don't care if you work or not, if you'd rather wear a gun or a teddy to bed, if you talk about nothing but criminals or babies, sit on your butt eating chocolate and gaining weight, or if you're out running down bad guys. I don't want to live without you."

Charlie burst into tears. "You're proposing to me while you're lying in a hospital bed?"

"I'd rather have been in front of you on bended knee, but I imagine you'll have me in that position soon enough." He winked.

It took a moment for Charlie to catch his suggestive meaning. "Ha. Okay. Just remember that while you're down there..."

Seth guffawed then bent forward with a groan. "Ow. That hurt. Don't make me laugh." He recovered then gave her a serious look. "Does that mean yes?"

"Of course it does!" Charlie rose to throw herself on top of him, mindful of his wounds and the oxygen tube. "I love you—I love you—I love you!" She kissed him on the lips, the cheeks, his eyelids and forehead.

They remained like that, holding hands and kissing one another, until it seemed Seth was having trouble breathing. Charlie moved away apologetically. She sniffed again and wiped her face, which was drenched with tears. "I'm a mess."

"You're beautiful." His eyes shone with love.

"I don't see how you can find me attractive," Charlie confessed, not fishing for a compliment. "This has been the worst day of my life, and I show it."

Seth sighed. "I'm feeling the painkillers they gave me right before you came in. Maybe it's time we called Sam in here while I still have the strength to ask his permission to marry you."

Charlie nodded and motioned for her father to join them. When Sam entered the room, she beamed. "Daddy, Seth wants to talk to you. And if you say no, I'll kill you."

"WHAT ARE YOU LOOKING AT?" Charlie knew her tone was cranky, but she had the worst case of wedding day jitters she could imagine.

Julio put his hands in his tux pockets. "No offense, but I've never seen you in a dress."

"So?" Now she was not only a sourpuss, but snappish.

"No dress means I've not seen your legs—I was beginning to think they were made of wood or titanium or something since you've always been such a hard ass." Julio's face reflected mild amusement.

Charlie stuck out her tongue. "You wouldn't be looking at my legs now if I wasn't bent over and didn't have my head between them. I don't want to ruin my gown. I'm ready to upchuck, and I haven't eaten anything all morning. And here you are, standing in as my maid of honor, and all you can do is make jokes about my body?"

"Your disposition, *querida,* not your form." He flashed her a toothy smile, his eyes twinkling. "You look adorable. If Seth hadn't already grabbed you, I'd whisk you away on my motorcycle and show you what you're missing by not being with a hot-blooded Latino."

Charlie clutched her stomach. She didn't dare risk laughing for fear she'd get sick. The dress wasn't tight, but she wasn't used to wearing anything with a cinched waist that showed off her cleavage and curves. She felt like a doll, waiting for someone to undress her and put her back into casual slacks and pullover shirts.

Julio took her by the hand and led her to the cheval mirror in his parents' dressing room. He'd talked Charlie into saying her vows at their country estate south of Houston. The setting was perfect. Spring flowers and trees blooming, a riot of color and greenery outside where the ceremony was to take place. A lovely master suite where Charlie could prepare for her wedding.

"Look," he said, helping right her and pointing at the mirror. "Don't you know how beautiful you are, and that Seth wouldn't care if you were wearing jeans as long as you showed up in front of that preacher?"

Charlie had to admit he was right. She'd never looked better. Weeks of work without hassle, days of being pampered at the best salon and day spa in Houston, courtesy of Julio. Stress-free and happier than she'd ever been.

She glanced at their reflection. He was grinning widely. His bandages, like Seth's, were gone, leaving scars from where he'd been shot. They were all lucky to be alive.

"Feel better?" he asked when she sighed deeply.

"Yeah." Charlie nodded. She looked more closely at their reflection. He'd had so many stitches and an operation to remove shrapnel from his head, so he'd kept it completely shaved. "How's the noggin'?"

He turned her to face him. "Look at me. I'm fine. Stop worrying about me. I hear your father outside talking to my dad. Did you catch what they said?"

She shook her head.

Julio held up a finger. "Hear it? The organist has started her music. It's time for us to go downstairs." He offered her his good arm.

A soft rap on the door...her father's voice asking if she was ready. Charlie took a deep gulp of air and blew it out slowly. "Let's do this."

SETH HAD BARELY NOTICED when Julio took his place in the garden where normally a bridesmaid or maid of honor would have stood. At first, when Charlie had asked Julio to be her closest witness to their marriage, it had seemed strange, but then nothing about Charlie could be considered the norm, and it was fitting that her partner stand beside her today, even though she had friends who could have done so.

All he could see was his beautiful bride, walking on her father's arm toward him, toward their future. He swelled with pride. His best friend, his soul mate, the love of his life. With Bill Stone as his best man, a small group of friends and family as witnesses, and him as ready as ever, the day was perfect. Life, for one brief moment in time, was perfect.

The words they both uttered, the clergy's needless encouragement for them to love and honor one another, the music…everything fell away, and Seth felt as if he was in a wonderful trance, leaving a troubled past behind and walking into a future bright with promise and passion.

Then he blinked. It was real, all right, but his bride's words… Seth couldn't believe what he'd heard. He played them over in his mind like a recording.

"I, Charlene Andrea Vargas, take you…Seth Benjamin Taggart, and whatever aliases you may have… as my lawfully wedded husband."

Members of those seated in the garden sniggered. Her father choked, coughed, recovered. Her mother gasped and closed her eyes with embarrassment, and Julio chuckled. Seth bit back a grin, but it was of no use. Charlie blinked through tears of laughter and smiled up at him, heart in her eyes, a mischievous smile on her lips.

And when it came time for him to kiss his bride, Seth swooped her into his arms and planted the biggest, most heartfelt kiss he'd ever given on her lips, crushing her to him, wedding gown and all, his soul bursting with pleasure.

The music started, and typical of Charlie, she'd surprised him by asking for something other than "The Bridal March." Seth laughed as he heard the fast-paced strains of an old cop show theme song being played on the organ. He could even imagine the drums, the trumpets and gigantic waves crashing all around them.

"Are you announcing to everyone where we're going on our honeymoon?" he teased, kissing the tip of her nose.

"Dad and Julio will be the only ones who get it." Charlie grabbed his arm and led him through a shower of rose petals and rice that pelted them on their quick-paced exit from the ceremony to the reception dinner.

Seth clasped her hand in his, grinning as Julio and Sam started laughing and the rest of the crowd cheered. Half of those who'd witnessed their wedding were cops, and Charlie was wrong—most of them seemed to catch the significance of the song.

"Book it, Danno!" called Sam as the theme from *Hawaii Five-O* filled the air.

EPILOGUE

MONTHS LATER, Seth watched the news on television as Charlie divested herself of gun, badge and purse. He motioned for her to join him.

"Come here. It's Dorinda and her husband. They're on the news."

"Your sister?" she teased.

"Aldridge's sister, thank you." He popped her on the butt as she perched on the edge of his chair and draped an arm about his shoulders.

The Associated Press's coverage was on the clandestine transporting of terrorists from Guatemala to the States, and Dorinda and Doug Wilkerson were front and center of the investigation.

"Oh, my." Charlie leaned forward. "Did they just say murder?" She chortled. "So that's what happened to the real Aldridge. They killed him and fed his body to the sharks, only gold fillings in dental records don't lie."

"Looks like they're bartering," Seth told her. "Copping to the murder in hopes of being sent back to the States—they don't want to spend their time in a Mexican prison. That doesn't work unless he was killed here, though, does it?"

She shook her head. "I suppose it beats having a Mexican execution or whatever the hell they do now for transporting terrorists." Charlie bent to kiss her husband of three months. "I still can't believe some of those arrested escaped from jail."

"Don't be so sure of their abilities," Seth told her. "I hear there's a new boy on the case, one who knows them and has a grudge."

"Who?" she asked.

Seth shook his head. "I'll tell you later. Right now I want to molest my wife. I haven't seen her for over eight hours."

Charlie loved it when Seth referred to her as his wife. She'd never be a domestic diva, but then her husband treated her more like a mistress than he did a housekeeper. Sure, they both did housework and attended to life's mundane aspects, but they talked. More than that, they communicated, and he spoke her language.

Seth had regained enough of his memory and physical strength to stay with his department, but he was no longer a field agent, which suited them both. Somebody needed to have the ability to work from home occasionally in case Sam was unavailable as babysitter to the child who was on the way.

"Aargh! You know I hate secrets." She punched him on the arm.

"But you love surprises." Seth yanked her into his arms, wrestling her and pinning her beneath him.

Before Charlie could question him further about

Rogers and other of his men who had escaped, their front doorbell rang.

"Julio!" she cried, throwing open the door to embrace him. She couldn't help but laugh when she saw the Mohawk sported by her former partner.

He grinned broadly and hugged her back. "I called earlier, and Seth said it was okay for me to come by before I left."

"You're leaving? Where? You're not well enough."

"I'm okay to travel."

"Nah." Charlie shook her head. "I know you too well. Travel, how? On that motorcycle of yours?"

He shrugged. "That's part of it."

Charlie frowned. "But your head and your shoulder!"

He patted his shoulder. "Another two weeks, and doctor says I'll be good as new. I'll just have a hole and a scar." He clucked his tongue against his teeth and winked. "I hear war wounds drive women wild." He rubbed the scar on his forehead and leaned forward. "Wanna touch the hair?"

"Yeah." Charlie couldn't help but giggle. "But why a Mohawk? Why not just stay bald or let the whole thing grow out?"

"It's for my new assignment—I'm going undercover. Didn't Seth tell you? He's the one who recommend me for the job, he and Stone."

Charlie drew a deep breath and looked accusingly at her husband. "Oh, really?"

"Yeah," Julio enthused. "I'm on special loan to

the Feds to help bring in Damien Rogers, that rat bastard. Since I'm familiar with the case, know what he looks like—I should. Was staring right at him when he had those goons in the rafters shoot at me. I figure I owe him something, you know? He shouldn'ta messed with Jorge and Maria's little boy."

Julio stabbed a thumb to his chest, indicating himself. Then he snapped his fingers. "Which reminds me, will you two look in on them, on my folks, while I'm gone? Just check, make sure they're okay?"

Charlie assured him that they would. "How long will you be gone?"

Julio shrugged. "Dunno. Maybe a month or two? A year? As long as it takes. I don't want to kill him—okay, maybe I do a little. But I want him to suffer. I want to bring him to justice and parade him down to wherever they send him myself."

"Hurt him once for me," she said.

"Will do, mamacita." He eyed her stomach. "Maybe I'll get back in time for Little Charlie's christening, no?"

Seth came up to stand behind Charlie. "You'd better. Mohawk and all."

Julio shook hands with Seth and hugged Charlie once more. "Well, I have some form of orientation tomorrow. Gotta hit the sack early tonight, so I'll see you later."

After the door shut behind Julio, Seth turned Charlie to face him and nuzzled her neck, nibbling the tender skin just behind her ear. "Honey, do you remember handcuffing me in Mexico?"

"Mm. You said you weren't mad about that anymore."

"I lied." Seth kissed her while walking her to the credenza where she'd unloaded her belongings after work. He found her handcuffs and told her to hold out her wrists. Snapping the first cuff to her and the second to himself, he started toward their bedroom, all the while telling her all the deliciously naughty things he was going to do to her once they were there.

Their front door opened suddenly, and there was a flurry of body parts as Charlie tried hiding her cuffed wrist behind her back and Seth attempted the same thing, only to yank her into him.

Julio didn't appear to notice at first, and he was still in a chatty mood. "I meant to tell you that my parents are hosting a party on the twelfth at—" He paused, eyeing them suspiciously as the couple tried to hide what they'd been doing.

Julio laughed. "Whazzup, partner? Is this man holding you against your will?"

Charlie flushed with embarrassment. "I—uh—that is, he was showing me a new maneuver."

Julio snorted. "Whatever." He waggled a finger at them. "I knew the two of you were kinkier than spiral pasta."

"Goodbye, Julio!" Seth and Charlie chorused.

Their friend held up his hands in surrender. "Just

sayin'…I'll be glad to help if you get into a bind." He cackled at his own joke. Then he snapped his fingers. "I'll email you the details about the party. Looks like you two were busy when I came in, and I know when I'm not wanted." He winked and shut the door behind him as he left.

Seth's eyes danced with laughter. "I don't believe I've ever seen you so shy. The unflappable Charlene Vargas, blushing like a bride."

"The name is Charlene Taggart," she informed him, tiptoeing to kiss his chin. "And I am a bride."

"Then let's start treating you like one, wife." Seth kissed her soundly.

Warmth flooded Charlie as her body melded with Seth's. His arms were sure and strong, his hands both possessive and caressing.

Wife. She liked the sound of that.

* * * * *

REQUEST YOUR FREE BOOKS!

2 FREE NOVELS
PLUS 2 FREE GIFTS!

WORLDWIDE LIBRARY®

Your Partner in Crime

YES! Please send me 2 FREE novels from the Worldwide Library® series and my 2 FREE gifts (gifts are worth about $10). After receiving them, if I don't wish to receive any more books, I can return the shipping statement marked "cancel." If I don't cancel, I will receive 4 brand-new novels every month and be billed just $5.24 per book in the U.S. or $6.24 per book in Canada. That's a saving of at least 34% off the cover price. It's quite a bargain! Shipping and handling is just 50¢ per book in the U.S. and 75¢ per book in Canada.* I understand that accepting the 2 free books and gifts places me under no obligation to buy anything. I can always return a shipment and cancel at any time. Even if I never buy another book, the two free books and gifts are mine to keep forever.

414/424 WDN FEJ3

Name (PLEASE PRINT)

Address Apt. #

City State/Prov. Zip/Postal Code

Signature (if under 18, a parent or guardian must sign)

Mail to the **Reader Service:**

IN U.S.A.: P.O. Box 1867, Buffalo, NY 14240-1867

IN CANADA: P.O. Box 609, Fort Erie, Ontario L2A 5X3

Not valid for current subscribers to the Worldwide Library series.

Want to try two free books from another line?
Call 1-800-873-8635 or visit www.ReaderService.com.

* Terms and prices subject to change without notice. Prices do not include applicable taxes. Sales tax applicable in N.Y. Canadian residents will be charged applicable taxes. Offer not valid in Quebec. This offer is limited to one order per household. All orders subject to credit approval. Credit or debit balances in a customer's account(s) may be offset by any other outstanding balance owed by or to the customer. Please allow 4 to 6 weeks for delivery. Offer available while quantities last.

Your Privacy—The Reader Service is committed to protecting your privacy. Our Privacy Policy is available online at www.ReaderService.com or upon request from the Reader Service.

We make a portion of our mailing list available to reputable third parties that offer products we believe may interest you. If you prefer that we not exchange your name with third parties, or if you wish to clarify or modify your communication preferences, please visit us at www.ReaderService.com/consumerschoice or write to us at Reader Service Preference Service, P.O. Box 9062, Buffalo, NY 14269. Include your complete name and address.

WWL11B